A Chance Inheritance

Carolyn Brown

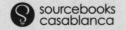

sourcebooks
casablanca

To my friend,
Sharon Sala

A Chance Inheritance © 2021, 2023 by Carolyn Brown
The Third Wish © 2017, 2023 by Carolyn Brown
Cover and internal design © 2023 by Sourcebooks
Cover design by Elsie Lyons
Cover images © Agnes Kantaruk/Shutterstock

Sourcebooks and the colophon are registered trademarks of Sourcebooks.

Published by Sourcebooks Casablanca, an imprint of Sourcebooks
P.O. Box 4410, Naperville, Illinois 60567-4410
(630) 961-3900
sourcebooks.com

A Chance Inheritance was originally published in 2021 by Audible Originals.
The Third Wish was originally self-published in 2017.

Printed and bound in Canada.
MBP 10 9 8 7 6 5 4 3 2 1

Chapter 1

LAINIE CORNELL WAS A REAL RUNAWAY BRIDE. She had crawled out the window of the country club, gotten into her car, and driven all the way from Dallas to Houston before she stopped and finally answered her father's call.

She had no doubts that she was doing the right thing. When it came right down to it, she didn't love Eli, and she hated the way he tried to dominate her. But to wait until the minute she was to walk down the aisle was unforgivable. She knew that.

Her two cousins, Becky and Jodi, had been her bridesmaids, and they had already made their way down the aisle to the front of the church when Lainie decided to run.

She promised herself that she would call each of them and apologize for embarrassing them so badly, but not until a couple of days had passed. It would take that long for Becky to stop cussing loud enough to melt the stained-glass windows in the church. Jodi would be angry for maybe the rest of the day and a night, but then she would understand, or at least Lainie thought she would. No doubt about it though, today was not the time to try to explain why she had taken off to any of them.

She checked into the cheap, no-tell motel still wearing her wedding dress, but she had tossed the veil and bouquet out the window somewhere south of Waco.

She answered the twentieth—or was it the twenty-fifth?—call from her father.

"Hello, Daddy," she said. "I just couldn't marry Eli even if—"

When her father was angry, he whispered. She could barely hear him when he said, "Wherever you are, you have responsibilities, so get your ass home."

"I've got to get things sorted out," she said. "I'll come back to Dallas when I—"

"You *will* come back right now," her father butted in before she could finish.

She ended the call and turned off her phone for two days. When she turned it back on, she had four missed calls and two voicemail messages from her cousin Becky telling her that Granny Lizzie's will had been read and that Lainie had inherited one-third of both the Catfish Fisherman's Hut and Granny Lizzie's house, which was located right beside it. She dried her eyes, forced herself to stop crying, and called Becky.

Lainie told her cousin she'd be there before supper, and then she took a quick shower, got dressed in jeans and a T-shirt, and picked up the garment bag holding her wedding dress and took it out to her car first. The thing filled the whole back seat. She didn't ever plan on wearing it again, but she just couldn't leave it behind. She went back inside her dingy little room and hauled out her two hot-pink suitcases, which contained everything she needed for a honeymoon in the Colorado mountains. The third trip back into the room was just to make sure she hadn't left anything behind.

Before she left, she checked her reflection in the mirror on the back of the bathroom door. Her black hair still had droplets of water hanging on her ponytail, and her green eyes had dark circles around them. She should stop by Dallas and try to explain how she felt to Eli, but her hands trembled at the thought of facing him.

"Oh, well, it doesn't matter if I look like crap. I'm going to Catfish, Texas, to work in a bait shop. I'm not having dinner tonight with the queen, not even if Becky acts like she is royalty." She left the room key on the nightstand and locked the door behind her, got into her little red sports car, and headed north toward the Red River.

"I love you, Granny Lizzie," Lainie sobbed as she drove. "Why did you have to die right before my wedding? I needed you to be there to tell me that marriage was tough enough when a woman loves a man, and impossible if she doesn't."

I was there in spirit, and I think you got the message. The voice in Lainie's head was as clear as if her grandmother had been sitting right beside her.

She didn't like the idea of working in the Catfish Fisherman's Hut or living with her two older, bossy cousins, but that was better than going back to Dallas. She hadn't even gotten out of Houston when the phone rang. She sucked in a lungful of air and hit the accept button.

"Hello, Daddy," she said. "I'm on my way to Granny Lizzie's place. She's left it to us three girls."

"That's probably for the best," he said. "Your mother has been crying one minute and then yelling the next since you ran away. She can't even hold her head up at the country club. You've made a mess of things, Lainie. You could have had such a good life with Eli, so it seems fitting that you have to live on the river in little more than a slum. It would be best if you call before you come back to see us. Give us time to forgive you for embarrassing the hell out of us."

"Yes, sir," she said and ended the call.

She was almost to Conroe when her phone rang again. This time it was Eli, and she let it ring four times before she finally answered.

"I'm very disappointed and upset." Eli's big, booming voice startled her. "Why did you run away? I deserve an answer."

"I figured out that I don't love you," she answered.

"Couldn't you have figured it out a hell of a lot earlier?" His tone was so icy that it sent a shiver down Lainie's spine.

"I did, but you are so controlling that you wouldn't..." She pulled off at the next exit to get a cup of coffee.

"I wouldn't what?" Eli demanded.

"Have let me break up with you," she finished. "It's over. I'm sorry I embarrassed everyone, but

I'm not sorry I left. Goodbye." She ended the call before he could say anything else.

"Granny understands why I ran away," Lainie told herself as she parked and ran into the Love's store for a cup of coffee. "I'll try to suck it up and not gag at the smell of fish bait, but I'm not making any promises about getting along with Becky and Jodi. It would have been so much better if Granny Lizzie had left me money instead of a beer, bait, and bologna shop. Then I could have opened my own little restaurant anywhere other than Dallas and could have been happy working sixteen hours a day."

Her phone rang just as she hit the Dallas noon traffic. When Becky's name came up on the screen, Lainie sighed loudly, pushed the accept button, and said, "Hello, how are things in Catfish?"

"Jodi and I have been here since last night. I opened up the shop this morning, and everything is in a mess. Jodi is still in the house trying to get awake. Where in the hell are you?" Becky's tone was covered with a thick layer of ice.

"Coming through Dallas," Lainie answered. "According to the GPS, I should be there by two o'clock."

"Well, don't fart around," Becky said. "I've decided

that we'll each take two days a week to open up the store at six in the morning, and whoever opens up can leave at three in the afternoon."

"What gives you the right to make the rules?" Lainie asked.

"I'm the oldest, and I got here first, and I've been here at the shop since six this morning, and Jodi still isn't here and it's noon, and Granny Lizzie made me executor over everything," Becky answered. "Do you need any more than that?"

"Who's going to kick Jodi out of bed at five thirty so she can get to the store by six on her two days?" Lainie asked.

"That's your job," Becky answered.

"You better think again on that issue. She's always been a bear in the mornings, but we can talk about it when I get there," Lainie said.

"Fair enough," Becky said. "Be safe."

"I'll do my best," Lainie said.

Jodi's alarm had gone off at five thirty that morning, but she hadn't even opened her eyes. She had just slapped it and gone right back to sleep. In ten minutes, it sounded again, so she reached down and unplugged the damned thing. When Becky beat on her door and demanded that she get up, she put a pillow over her head. After the first three times her phone rang, she turned it off.

Her internal clock awoke her at noon, just like always. For the past ten years, she'd worked as a beautician in a salon in Walmart that stayed open until ten o'clock at night. Her shift went from one to ten, so she was used to partying after work until the bars shut down and then sleeping until noon. If Becky expected her to get up before daylight, she had rocks for brains.

The only noise in the house was the sound of the window air-conditioning unit in the living room kicking on and off, and from outside the crunch of gravel on tires from cars and trucks passing by on their way to the store or the Red River. Somehow, the house had seemed bigger when she and her two cousins were kids. The place had a small living room, a tiny kitchen, and two bedrooms. One had been Granny Lizzie's, and the other one had two sets of bunk beds in it.

Most of the time the cousins all came at the same time in the summer. Becky and Jodi were older than Lainie, so they claimed the top bunks, and she had to sleep on a bottom one. She whined about it, but then Lainie had always been the prissy one of the three of them. Jodi would have never thought that she would have the nerve to be a runaway bride.

Jodi rolled out of bed and stumbled across the hall to the bathroom. She brushed kinky blond hair up into a messy bun, and then headed to the kitchen. The coffeepot was still half-full, so she poured a mugful, heated it up in the microwave, and sat down at the table with it.

"At least Becky can't fire me for being late," she mumbled. In ten years she'd worked under three different owners at the beauty salon in Carrollton, Texas, and just last week the newest manager had fired her for being late too many times. "This place is one-third mine. If I choose to work my one-third of the day in the afternoon and evening, then it's my choice."

The house phone that hung on the wall right behind her head rang and startled her so badly that she spilled coffee all over her faded nightshirt. She picked up the receiver and said, "What do you want, Becky? You just made me dump a whole cup of hot coffee on my favorite shirt."

"Did it burn you too bad to come to work?" Becky asked.

"No, it had cooled down a little. I told you when I first got here that I wasn't getting up at that ungodly hour of the morning, so you can get your panties out of the wad they're twisted up in and accept it. Where's Lainie? Is she going to run out on us like she did the wedding? That was embarrassing, standing up there waiting and no bride coming down the aisle on Uncle John's arm, wasn't it?"

"Stop trying to sidestep the issue. Get dressed and come to the store. The coffeepot out here stays full all day, so you can have your morning cup when you get to work. There's breakfast sandwiches in the freezer, so you can heat one of those in the microwave. This is the first day we've been open since Granny Lizzie died. It's a mess, and customers are swarming the place. So, get your lazy ass in gear," Becky said and hung up the phone.

Jodi reached behind her and put the receiver back where it belonged. She stood to her feet, whipped around, and saluted the gold-colored phone. "Yes, ma'am! I'll get right on that, ma'am. Anything else you want to yell at me about, General Becky?"

She took a quick shower, tossed her nightshirt

and the dirty clothing she'd brought with her in a garbage bag into the washing machine, and then got dressed in a pair of khaki shorts and a clean shirt. The phone rang as she was leaving the house, but she didn't answer it.

"I'm on my way," she muttered. "At least General Becky can't fire me."

She walked across the yard, through the gate, and crossed the parking lot to the store. The name of the place, the Catfish Fisherman's Hut, had been painted on the window more than fifty years ago when Granny Lizzie's parents owned the place. A picture of a huge channel catfish arched above the logo. Both were faded these days, but still legible.

"I bet that catfish doesn't give a good hot damn if I'm late," Jodi muttered as she climbed the steep steps to the wooden porch. The store, like the house, was set up on six-foot stilts with an open-air space underneath. The Red River had flooded its banks lots of times in the past, but so far it hadn't reached the floorboards of the store or the house. Jodi swiped a tear from her cheek when she thought of all the times her job at the end of the evening had been to line up the old ladder-back chairs that were now scattered all over the long porch. She took a moment to get them in order and to swallow the lump in her throat before she went inside.

The paint was chipped on every one of the chairs, showing that they had been painted red, orange, and even black before the final yellow coat had been applied. She stood back and looked at the last chair and then opened the door. The bell above it dinged and the store went surprisingly silent as everyone turned to look at her.

"Good mornin'," she said. "Can I help someone find something?"

The silence went from so quiet that they could have heard a catfish swimming down the river to a steady buzz of conversation. Becky pointed to the cash register, and Jodi nodded. She would far rather ring up sales and take money than dip up minnows or help someone find just the right stink bait or box of worms. Becky was the one who had enjoyed fishing when they were kids and had loved to help Granny Lizzie dip the minnows from the long, narrow tank at the back of the store. Jodi would far rather hide under the shade of the big weeping willow trees and read a book.

The two women were swamped for an hour, and then the store cleared out enough that she could grab a root beer and a candy bar. She perched on a barstool behind the checkout counter and twisted the top off her soda pop. "You really meant it when you said we were busy," she said.

Becky poured herself a cup of coffee and hopped up onto the counter. "Did you think I was just BS-in' you? I don't know how Granny Lizzie ran this place by herself."

Before Jodi could respond, Lainie pushed open the door and said, "Hello, I'm here."

"Surprise, surprise," Becky said. "We thought you might run out on us like you did your wedding a week ago."

"Do you even know how embarrassing that was for us?" Jodi barely gave Becky time to finish before she lit into Lainie. "I was even on time, which was doing good for me, and there me and Becky were at the front of the church. The "Wedding March" started, and your dad came down the aisle alone."

"Hey, don't give me any crap," Lainie said. "I can always go right back outside and leave. I haven't unloaded my bags at the house yet. I came straight here."

Becky chuckled. "Where are you going to go? You quit your job. Aunt Melanie and Uncle John are mad at you, so get off your high horse and get ready to work."

"I'm not on a high horse, and for your information, I was standing there waiting for Daddy to knock on the dressing room door when I figured out that I loved my wedding dress and all the presents more than I loved Eli, and..." She stopped and sucked in a lungful of air. "He was so controlling that I was having trouble breathing. He expected to tell me where to go, what to wear, and how to style my hair. I just couldn't see waking up next to him every morning for the rest of my life and putting up with him ordering me around like he'd been doing." Lainie crossed her arms over her chest. "Now what do you want me to do, and can I at least grab a doughnut and a bottle of chocolate milk before I start?"

Jodi shot a look toward Becky.

"Why are you looking at me?" Becky asked.

"I told you she had a good reason," Jodi answered and then focused on Lainie. "I can't believe that you didn't call it off weeks before the wedding, when you felt like that."

"It had gone too far, or so I thought. Daddy is even more furious with me than I thought he would be." Lainie shrugged.

"Way to go, Lainie, but I'm wondering why *you* are here, Becky?" Jodi asked. "You had a cushy job in that big oil company."

"I got tired of working with Derrick, my ex-boyfriend. We've been apart for two years, but working with him was a nightmare," Becky said. "Granny Lizzie leaving this place to us was a godsend."

"Amen," Lainie said.

"Another amen from me," Becky declared. "And yes, Lainie, you can grab a snack before you start stocking shelves. There's several boxes in the storeroom that need to be put out. I didn't have time to get any of that kind of thing done and wait on customers, too. Now that we're all three here"—she shot a look over at Jodi—"maybe we can get this place organized."

Jodi finished her candy bar and carried her root beer to the storeroom, where boxes of merchandise were stacked against every wall. "Sweet Jesus! Didn't Granny Lizzie unpack anything for the last month?"

Becky followed her into the room. "This is a busy season, and after running this place all by myself all morning, I'd say that she didn't have the time to even think about unpacking chips and bread."

Then the waterworks started, and Becky slumped to the floor and wept like a baby.

Jodi couldn't let anyone cry alone, so she dropped to her knees beside her cousin, draped an arm around her shoulders, and sobbed with her. "I'm sorry I didn't come help you this morning."

"That's not why"—Becky took several long gulps of air—"I'm shedding tears. It's just that the three of us used to play in this room, and I could almost see her bringing us root beers and candy"— she covered her face with her hands—"back here, and then rushing out front to wait on customers."

Lainie sat down on the other side of Becky and patted her on the back. "I'd forgotten that until…" She wiped the first tears from her cheeks. "Dammit! I thought I'd gotten all cried out this week when I heard she'd died just days before my wedding. Granny Lizzie wouldn't want us to be doing this. She'd want us to come in here like a bulldozer and take control."

"I know that's what she would want, but I miss her so much," Jodi wailed. "That's why I didn't want to wake up and come out here this morning. Being in the house is tough, but we spent weeks every summer running in and out of this store."

Becky took a deep breath, dried her eyes on the tail of her T-shirt, and stood up. "All right, girls. We've had our good cry for the day. Now, it's time to suck it up and go to work. Lainie is right. Granny Lizzie would throw a hissy fit if she saw us acting like this."

"Oh, yeah, she would," Lainie agreed as she got to her feet and held out a hand to help Jodi. "The Cornell girls are here to kick butt and make Granny Lizzie proud of us."

"It's just a store," Chris Adams told himself over and over as he drove the last five miles from his place to the Catfish Fisherman's Hut. The dirt road had a fresh layer of gravel in some places, ruts and holes in others, but it was the only way to get to Lizzie's, as the local folks called the bait shop that sat right on the Red River.

"I wonder if the three granddaughters will change the name of the place to Catfish Fisherperson's Hut." He grinned, but it didn't last long. Lizzie Cornell would come right up out of her grave and give those girls a tongue-lashing if they tried to change the name. What society thought didn't matter a damn bit to her.

"My great-grandparents named this store when they built it at the turn of the century when the town of Catfish had three churches and that many brothels. All that's gone now, but my store will stand as long as there's a catfish in the Red River," she had told him.

The memory of her voice filled his eyes with tears, but he blinked them away. Lizzie wouldn't want him bawling like a baby over her. She had been a surrogate grandmother as well as a good friend to him through the past two decades that he'd lived in the area. His own parents had died when he was seven years old, and his grandfather, a fishing guide who had taught him the business, had taken him to raise.

Buster Adams was a gruff old guy, but he was fair, and he made sure that Chris graduated from high school before he turned the business over to him. He had passed away five years ago. Chris had scattered his ashes out in the middle of the Red River just like he had been told to do. Lizzie was the only one he'd asked to sit beside him in the boat that day. She had said a few words, and then they had cried together.

Chris parked his old work truck beside the three

others sitting in front of the store and took a deep breath. "It's just a store," he reminded himself again. "Becky might not even be here today."

When he opened the door and slid out of the vehicle, two old fishermen waved from the porch. One of them motioned him to the porch with a flick of his wrist and said, "Come on in. The girls are here, so we don't need to work. There's a pot of coffee brewing. It's not quite as strong as what Lizzie brewed, but it's not bad."

Chris climbed the steps up to the porch that had been set up on six-foot stilts. In his lifetime the river had flooded three times, and if it hadn't been for the posts keeping both the store and Lizzie's house up off the ground, she would have lost them both.

Rosco, a short little man without a hair on his head, pointed to the chair beside him. "The girls have finally all made it. The last one just got here about two hours ago."

Orville, a tall lanky guy who fished off the pier with Rosco every day that it didn't rain, lowered his voice. "If they decide livin' out here in the sticks is not their cup of tea, me and Rosco is goin' to make them an offer to buy the place. We ain't got a lick of business sense, but we was hopin' you'd partner up with us, since you're smart when it comes to all that. We can't let this place close up for good."

"Maybe one of them will keep it going." Chris sat down, and half a dozen cats came up from under the porch. "Hello, Angels." He chuckled as he bent forward and rubbed each of their ears. "I'll save you some fish heads if we catch anything today."

"Lizzie was smart when it came to her cats," Rosco chuckled. "Just call them all Angel. Then when one died or one showed up, she didn't have to worry with rememberin' names."

"Lizzie was smart about everything." Orville nodded. "If she hadn't intimidated the hell out of me, I would have asked her out on a date a year after Everett died."

Rosco bent down and stroked a tabby cat from head to tail. "I thought about it, but I didn't have the nerve either. So..." He sighed. "You got a guidin' job today, Chris, or are you just fishin' for fun and food?"

"I've got a job," Chris answered. "I should go on in and get my supplies for the trip. My guys are supposed to show up about six to do some night fishin'. Y'all catch anything today?"

"Got a two-pound channel cat that me and

Rosco skinned and cut up into fillets and ate right out there on the sandbar," Orville said. "Went down right good with that six-pack of cold beer we shared. Now neither one of us has to cook supper."

"I should get on in there and gather up what I need and get the beer and sandwich meat in the cooler." Chris continued to pet a black-and-white cat. He knew he was dragging his feet because Becky was probably in the store, but he wasn't ready to see her just yet. What could he say to her about her grandmother? "I'm sorry for your loss, for all our loss" seemed trite and pretty damned cold.

Rosco stood up and groaned. "My knees hate these stairs, but my butt sure loves the chairs."

"That's because the imprint of your ass is in that chair you've been sittin' in for the last forty years. No wonder you can see all the layers of paint where the yellow is chipped away. You've wallowed them colors off," Orville teased, but he, too, moaned when he got to his feet. "It ain't my knees, but my hip. Doc says it should've been replaced years ago, but I ain't willin' to give up six weeks of fishin' to get it done. I'll see you tomorrow, Chris. Get on in there and lay your stake on one of them women. They're all good-lookin', and if you can hitch up with one, you might inherit the store with her."

"Hell, Orville, the store ain't worth havin' a naggin' woman over." Rosco handed him his cane and picked up his own. "You should know that, after them last two wives you had to divorce just so you could go fishin'."

Chris made sure both of the old guys made it down the steps before he opened the old wooden screen door and went into the store. When he stepped inside, he was overwhelmed with a fresh wave of sadness. He'd been in the place every day since Miz Lizzie died more than a week ago, but today the store looked even emptier without her standing behind the counter, her usual oversized mug of coffee in her hand.

"Well, well, well!" Jodi turned around and smiled. "If it's not the handsome Chris Adams who's coming into our store."

"Hello, Jodi," he said, but instead of looking at her, he was already scanning the place for Becky, his first love—even though she had no idea.

"Hey, Chris," Lainie said from over near the beer and soda pop. "How have you been?"

"Good," he answered.

Becky came out of the back room and smiled at him. "Chris, it's sure good to see you."

Was it really, or was that just something to say in an awkward situation? She hadn't changed much since he'd last seen her five years ago. In his eyes, she was still the most beautiful woman God ever dropped on earth. Blond hair and full lips that begged for kisses. A small waist that nipped in above well-rounded hips, and a smile so bright that it could make the sun hide behind a cloud.

"Good to see you too. I would have come to the funeral if there had been one," he said.

"I know"—Becky's big brown eyes floated with tears—"but we did it the way she wanted. As soon as they release her ashes, we'll scatter them out there in the Red River. She left orders in her will for us to do that, and we intend to take care of things just the way she wanted. Maybe you could be there when we do that."

"Just tell me when and where," he said.

"We sure will." Becky wiped her eyes on the sleeve of her shirt.

He wanted to take a few steps forward, wrap her up in his arms, and tell her that everything was going to be all right. But his feet were glued to the floor.

"What can we help you with today?" Jodi asked.

"I need three dozen minnows and some worms to start with," he said without taking his eyes off Becky.

"Are you still in the fishin' guide business?" Jodi asked.

"Yep, I am." He nodded. "I'll also need some bread, a couple of those packs of sandwich meat with several kinds in it, and a few bags of chips. Mix them up. I never know what the fishermen will like."

"I'll get that for you," Lainie said.

"I've got a list"—he pulled it from his shirt pocket—"if you could fill it for me."

Lainie took it from his hand. "Glad to do that. Grab a cup of coffee while I get it ready. Won't take me but a few minutes."

Chris made his way to the back of the store where the coffeepot was always going and poured a cupful. "So, you're all home now?"

"I'm not sure if it's home." Becky was only a few feet from him and was busy arranging cans of Vienna sausage and tuna fish on a shelf. "But we're all here until we figure out what to do."

"Think any of you will stay?" Chris set his coffee down on the table and helped her get the shelf filled.

"I'm plannin' on it," she answered.

His heart threw in an extra beat. Becky wasn't leaving. That meant maybe, just maybe, if she wasn't engaged or if she didn't have a boyfriend, he would have a chance this time.

"Don't know about those other two"—she nodded toward Lainie and Jodi—"but this is the only place I ever really felt at home, so I'm not going anywhere."

"I'll sure be here for a long time," Lainie said. "I haven't got anywhere to go, so I don't have a choice until Mama and Daddy get over their snit." She gathered up the items on his list and took them to the checkout counter.

"I was fired last week from my beauty shop job. The manager said I'd been late too many times, so I'm here for a little while anyway. I don't know what the big deal was. I didn't have anything on the books for thirty minutes after I arrived, but she wanted us all there when the place opened," Jodi said as she rang up the items Lainie brought to the front of the store.

"Miz Lizzie would like that you're all here," Chris said. "Need any more help?"

"That was the last box. I'm ready for a cold beer." Becky headed for the cooler and took out a long-neck bottle of Coors. "Want one? It can be payment for helping me."

"I'll take a rain check. The guys I'm guiding tonight will be here soon, so I should get on down to the boat and get things ready to go," Chris said. "Maybe another night."

"Anytime," Becky said.

Chapter 2

BECKY KICKED OFF HER SHOES JUST INSIDE THE door to the house, went straight to the window air-conditioning unit and set the temperature down, then collapsed on the sofa. "I cannot go to work at six o'clock every morning and work until ten. I just can't do it."

Lainie set her suitcases in the middle of the living room floor and eased down on the other end of the sofa. "I don't know how you did it even today. I'm exhausted after only eight hours at the store, and you've been on your feet for eighteen."

Jodi groaned as she sank down into an old wooden rocker. "I'm sorry I didn't get out there until after noon, so stop giving me those dirty looks."

"I've got an idea," Lainie said. "Becky is used to getting up at the crack of dawn to make the commute to her workplace, so she can open the store at six and work until two. That's eight hours. I go in at ten and work until six. That gives me eight hours.

Jodi comes in at two and works until closing at ten and that's her shift. Becky will be alone in the store for four hours in the morning, and Jodi will have the same amount of time in the evening."

"That means you will always have someone in the store with you," Jodi said.

Lainie raised a shoulder in half a shrug. "I'm the runner, remember? I'll need supervision."

Becky giggled. "Makes sense to me. During the busy part of the day, there will be two of us there. And when we're not busy, we can keep the shelves straightened up and the place in order, right?" She looked from Lainie to Jodi.

"Oh, so you're going to be a stickler." Lainie yawned. "I thought maybe Jodi and I would just sit on the stool behind the checkout counter and do our nails."

"You always were a smart-ass," Jodi said.

"And you were always the one who'd do anything to get out of work, and you were never on time. You want to trade times with me? I'll gladly work the two-to-ten shifts," Lainie threw back at her.

Jodi shook her head. "No, I'm fine with that schedule. I'm used to working those hours at the beauty shop."

Becky liked the new schedule Lainie had come up with, but right then she just wanted a shower to wash the fish smell off her skin and out of her hair, and to fall into a bed with soft sheets. "Since I'm the one getting up so early, I'll take Granny Lizzie's room."

"You can have it." Jodi shivered. "I cry every time I go in there."

"As long as I can have a bottom bunk, I don't care where I sleep. I'll use one of the top bunks for my wedding dress." Lainie stood up and headed back outside. "I still have to bring it in."

"You brought your dress?" Jodi raised both of her eyebrows.

Lainie turned around at the door. "Of course I brought it. I wouldn't leave a one-of-a-kind special designer dress behind in a cheap motel, and besides, we're all the same size. One of you might need to use it. I'm not blind. I saw the way you"— she pointed at Jodi—"were flirting with Chris."

Jodi shook her head. "Not me! No, sir! If you're expecting me to wear that dress, you can just take it straight to the river and give it a toss. I'm not getting married for years, if ever. Men are nothing but trouble. I might have flirted a little with Chris, but that was just for fun. Besides, any fool can see that he only has eyes for Becky. She's the one who'll need the dress."

"You're full of crap." Becky yawned. "Chris probably has a girlfriend, or maybe even a fiancée, and for your information, I'm not having a huge wedding. I'm finished with fancy stuff, and besides, that dress is unlucky. Lainie ran away in it," she said. "I'm taking a shower, and I'll be asleep before my head hits the pillow. Five thirty comes early. Good night."

"'Night," Lainie and Jodi said in unison.

A claw-foot tub took up most of one wall in the bathroom. When Becky was a little girl, Granny Lizzie would put all three girls in the tub at the same time after she'd closed up the store. After working all day, Becky had a brand-new appreciation for her grandmother's strength and energy. Now that she had some idea of what it required to take care of the store, Becky wondered why Granny Lizzie even wanted them to come spend part of the summer with her. She couldn't imagine having to see after three little girls and make sure they were cleaned up for bed after she'd closed up shop today.

Becky dropped her clothing on the floor, looked at the tub, and smiled at the memory of those long-ago summers. Granny Lizzie had had a shower installed in the corner of the bathroom, and tonight, in Becky's exhausted state, a shower was what she needed. The stall was tiny, but then Granny Lizzie had been smaller than any of her granddaughters, standing at five feet, two inches, and weighing maybe a hundred and ten pounds if she was soaking wet.

Becky adjusted the water, got inside, and pulled the shower curtain shut. She let the hot water beat down on her aching back muscles for a few minutes before she picked up the shampoo and washed her hair. After college, she had landed a job as an accountant in a huge oil company in Dallas. She'd worked eight hours a day for the past eight years, but she'd had a cubicle of her own, and she hadn't been on her feet sixteen hours a day. Still, if she had to work that many hours from now on, she would do it. Anything beat working at the same place as her ex and watching him flirt with every new woman who got hired.

"Besides, Granny Lizzie has put her trust in us girls to keep her bait store running. Even if the other two decide they don't want to stick around, I promise I'll keep it going. If they want to sell their share of the business and house to me, I'll use my savings to buy them out," she muttered as she worked shampoo into her hair.

She hadn't been in Granny Lizzie's room yet, and she thought she was ready for all the feelings that would hit her when she stepped through the door. But she was not. Emotions hit her from every side. The room still had the faint scent of her grandmother's perfume, L'Aimant by Coty. She'd worn it for years and years, and a bottle still sat on her dresser, along with pictures of all three of her granddaughters.

Becky stopped long enough to pick up each picture and look at it; then, with tears in her eyes, she pulled back the chenille bedspread and the sheet and crawled into bed. The ceiling became a Technicolor screen for flashes of memories of all the times when she had been in Catfish over the years. She had been six years old in the first one. Granny Lizzie had put her and four-year-old Jodi and Lainie, who was just a toddler, in the back room to play while she waited on customers. When Becky tried to boss the younger girls, they'd rebelled, and Granny Lizzie had to come back to settle the fuss. From there, it jumped ahead several years to when she was sixteen and realized that Chris Adams had a big crush on her, but she wasn't interested, and he never pushed the issue. He was a sweet kid, but at that age, Becky was so sure she wanted someone with more on the ball than being a fishing guide.

"Too smart for my own britches," she muttered as tears washed down the sides of her cheeks onto the pillow. She fell asleep thinking about the last five years. All three of them had come to Catfish on a day between Christmas and New Year's that suited all of them to spend time with Granny Lizzie. Little did they know when they all left three months ago that it would be the last time they'd ever see their grandmother.

Becky's eyes popped wide open the next morning at five thirty. She slung her legs over the side of the four-poster bed and sat there for a moment to get her bearings. Today was March 16. Yesterday was Monday, so this was Tuesday. She and her cousins had survived the Ides of March, and they hadn't killed each other. That was a good sign.

She didn't bother to make a pot of coffee at the house. The other two wouldn't be up and around for hours, and she could always have her first cup of the day at the store. She dressed and headed that way. When she arrived, Rosco and Orville were already on the porch and petting half a dozen cats.

"Good mornin'," Rosco said.

"Right on time." Orville grinned. "We ain't been waitin' long."

"Mornin' to both of you. Coffee should be ready in a few minutes. Think the fish will be bitin' today?" she asked as she unlocked the door and flipped on the lights.

"Yep, it's cloudy," Rosco answered.

"They're always hungrier when it's cloudy than when the sun is shining." Orville followed her inside. "You might as well get ready for a big crowd here in an hour or so."

Rosco came in right behind him. "Hey, Orville, she's got them little white doughnuts we like back on the shelf. I'm gettin' two packages to go with my coffee. You want some?"

"Nope, I'm having two honey buns this mornin'. The nice thing about gettin' old is that we can eat what we want." Orville sent a wink and a smile across the room to Becky.

"Good mornin', everyone. Coffee ready?" Chris said as he came into the store.

Becky whipped around and locked eyes with him. "In a minute, but what are you doing out this early?"

"I've got a married couple and their teenage son who want to go out today since it's cloudy. They'll be here at ten. Thought you might need some help until they get here," he answered. "This weather is going to bring out the fishermen by the dozens. I used to drop in and help Miz Lizzie all the time."

"I never turn down help." Becky smiled up at him and wondered why she'd been so stupid when she was a teenager.

"Where's the other two girls?" Rosco asked.

"They got their fill of hard work and lit a shuck for the big city, didn't they?" Orville asked.

"Nope, they'll be here later," Becky answered. "We worked out a schedule. I open up. Jodi closes shop at night. Lainie comes in and does a shift starting at ten in the morning so that during the busy part of the day, two of us will be here."

"You'll need extra help in the mornings on Tuesdays," Chris said. "Today is when the milkman delivers and the beer man makes it down this way. But don't worry, I'll be here." He'd get up early every day just to be near her for a few hours.

"Thank you." Becky nodded. "Coffee is just

about done dripping. I'll start a second pot and ring up whatever you want for breakfast."

"I'm right glad you're still lettin' the coffee be free," Orville said as he poured himself and Rosco each a cup. "Miz Lizzie would like that."

"We'll keep things just like she did." Becky rang up his pastries.

Chris held the door open for both of the old guys, and then went to the back of the store and filled two mugs. He carried them to the checkout counter and handed one to Becky. Their fingers brushed in the transfer, and sparks danced all around the fisherman's hut. Becky's hand trembled as she brought the mug to her lips for the first taste.

"Nothing like the first sip of coffee in the morning, is there?" Chris asked.

"You got it," Becky agreed. "I'm going to heat up a sausage biscuit in the microwave. Want one?"

"Sure." He nodded.

Why hadn't she realized all those years ago just how handsome he was? With his dirty-blond hair that was always a little too long and those clear blue eyes, he could probably have any woman in the state of Texas. Add in the fact that his broad chest and biceps stretched the knit of his shirt, and it was a wonder he didn't have women panting around after him like puppies.

She unwrapped four sausage biscuits and popped them into the microwave. When it dinged, she put them on a paper plate and set it on the counter. "Breakfast is served."

He picked one up and then looked over at her. "Thank you for making this for us. I hate eating alone."

"Me too, and you are welcome." She took her first bite.

"You said you were staying here." He waved a hand around to take in the whole store. "Did you quit your job?"

She nodded and swallowed, then took a sip of coffee. "I had two weeks' vacation time coming, so I took it and resigned effective after my vacation ended. I cleaned out my office and came straight here. I knew when I left that I wasn't going back. Granny Lizzie always talked about keeping this legacy going, and I intend to do just that."

She could have sworn that his eyes twinkled when he heard that. He couldn't possibly still have a crush on her after all this time—or could he?

Chapter 3

JODI AWOKE TO THE SOUND OF POTS AND PANS rattling in the kitchen. She barely opened one eye a slit and slammed a pillow over her head when she saw that it was only nine o'clock. Granted, she hadn't spent the night before having drinks with her friends at a bar, but she had read a steamy romance book until almost two in the morning. The aroma of cinnamon and bacon wafted down the short hallway, under the door, and straight to her nose.

"Well, hell's bells," she groaned as she sat up in the bunk bed and bumped her head. "Dammit!" She swore a second time as she grabbed her head and threw herself backward.

There was little use in trying to go back to sleep now, so she got up and wandered down the hall and into the small dining area. Lainie was humming in the galley kitchen as she made French toast. She'd already fried a plateful of bacon, and the coffee was made.

"You cook?" Jodi slumped down in a chair.

"You don't?" Lainie fired back at her.

"I can make a mean bologna sandwich, and I'm a master at frozen pizza in the microwave. Other than that, I know how to order out and pick it up at the window," Jodi yawned. "I like good food, but could you do it a little quieter from now on?"

"Nope," Lainie answered. "If you don't like noise in the kitchen, then use earplugs, or learn to go to bed by midnight." She set a plate of French toast and bacon in front of her cousin and poured her a cup of coffee. "When you taste my food, you'll be glad that I woke you up."

"What makes your stuff so great?" Jodi asked.

"That fancy chef at the fancy cooking school where I trained taught me well. I wanted to own my own restaurant, but then I met Eli." Lainie shrugged. "He asked me to quit my job, so I did. Then I realized that I didn't like the idea of being dependent on him. And now here I am cooking for you ungrateful cousins who would just as soon have heat-and-serve biscuits from the store."

"Don't be calling me ungrateful." Jodi did a head wiggle, and then took her first bite. "I like food, fancy or plain, and this is some good stuff, coz!"

She rolled her eyes appreciatively. "I should take your shift at the store, and you should just stay in this kitchen and cook for us."

"That wouldn't be fair to Becky." Lainie fixed herself a plate and sat down across from Jodi. "Besides, I'm not sure I want to be a chef anymore. I might just want to run a beer, bait, and bologna store. Do you want to fix hair the rest of your life?"

"I don't know what I want to do, but I do know that the only place I was ever really happy was right here when we visited Granny Lizzie," Jodi admitted. "Mother and Daddy were always arguing about something, and I grew up thinking it was my fault they couldn't get along. If you and Becky want to sell the place, I will buy your shares. I've got enough savings and good credit to put a down payment on the property. Maybe someday, I'll add a room onto the house, put in a beauty shop, and hire some help for the store."

Lainie shook her head. "I'm not selling a square inch of this place. I couldn't wait for summer so I could come stay with Granny Lizzie. My one regret is that after I was grown, I didn't come see her often enough. I should be ashamed for only being here twice a year, and even then, I didn't spend a night with her."

Jodi's eyes welled up, and the next bite of her French toast was hard to swallow. "I only came at Christmas the last five years. So, what are we going to do if none of us want to sell?"

"We'll live here and run the store together," Lainie said.

No clubs. No friends to hang out with after work. Just sleep, work, and smell minnows. Is that what you really want? the pesky voice in Jodi's head asked.

Today it is. I'll worry about tomorrow when it gets here. Besides, there's plenty of beer in the store, and I've got Becky and Lainie to hang out with, and maybe there's a good-lookin' fisherman in my future, Jodi argued.

"So, now that you're awake, what are you going to do between now and the time you go to work?" Lainie asked. "You're used to the city life with clubs and bars and lots of friends. It's over an hour's drive to the nearest place where you can get a drink, unless you want to get into the bottle of Jack Daniel's that Granny Lizzie keeps up in the cabinet."

Her voice broke into Jodi's thoughts and brought her back to the present. She cocked her head to one side and took a sip of coffee. "I might need a drink one of these evenings, so thanks for telling me it's up there, but right now, I'm going fishing. I bet you can do wonders with catfish or bass, right?"

"If you clean it and bring it to me in fillets"— Lainie nodded—"I could make it for supper after my shift at the store, but first you have to catch something."

"Don't you remember? I'm the fish whisperer," Jodi teased as she finished off her breakfast and headed down the hallway.

———————

The skies were almost solid gray when Lainie went down the porch steps and walked out across the yard toward the store. The faint smell of rain mixed with the pungent aroma of river water floated on the gentle breeze that stirred the minty-green leaves of the willow trees. She had to watch her step because two of Lizzie's Angels had come out from under the porch and followed her through the yard gate and the gravel parking lot. They left her at the bottom of the steps to rush under the store and fight with the other cats over a couple of fish heads.

"Y'all taking care of the Angels?" Lainie grinned

when she noticed Rosco and Orville in their usual chairs.

"Yep, we done caught enough for our dinner, so we're just havin' a midmornin' snack before we go home and cook 'em," Rosco answered.

"The Angels love their fresh fish, and we're doin' our part to keep them from sneakin' into the store and eatin' up all the minnows," Orville told her. "We saw Jodi down at the river. Why isn't she up here helpin' y'all in the store?"

"Remember? I told y'all that her shift doesn't begin until two," Lainie explained.

"Yep, you did." Orville chuckled. "Sometimes my old brain doesn't register real good."

"Miz Lizzie said y'all was smart girls." Rosco nodded. "Guess she was right. You done figured out a schedule so that none of you have to be here all day long. I hear vehicles comin' this way. Looks like y'all are about to get busy."

"Good thing I got here early." Lainie opened the door.

"We're like them Walmart greeters." Orville chuckled. "We'll make everyone welcome before they come inside, and then they'll be in a good mood and buy more."

Lainie turned around and flashed a bright smile at them. "Well, thank you, and we'll see to it that you get free coffee every day for all your hard work."

She rounded the end of the checkout counter, tucked her purse on the shelf underneath, and then made herself a tall disposable cup of sweet tea. "How did the morning go?"

Becky finished straightening a shelf and joined Lainie behind the counter. "Fast and furious until about ten minutes ago, but Chris showed up and helped me."

"Should we redo the schedule?" Lainie asked.

"I don't think so." Becky did a little hop and sat on the counter. "They tell me that so many fishermen are coming out today because it's cloudy. I guess we'll learn this business as we go."

"Speaking of that"—Lainie hiked a hip up on the barstool—"are you planning on selling your share or stickin' around? Jodi and I were talking about it over breakfast this morning, and we both plan on staying."

"I'm not giving up one little bit of our inheritance," Becky declared with enough conviction in her tone that Lainie believed her. "We are the fourth generation of Cornell women to own this store and the house. I was thinking I would buy you two out if you wanted to take your share and go back to the city."

"Not me." Lainie shook her head. "Think we can get along enough to run the business together?"

"I guess we'll find out," Becky answered. "I thought I'd take the books home with me when I leave this afternoon. I'd like to go over them, and then, when we're all together tonight, I'll tell you if we're starting out in the red, or if this place makes enough profit to support all three of us."

"And if it doesn't?" Lainie immediately began to think about her savings. If the bait shop couldn't make enough money to support them, then maybe she could work a night shift in a restaurant over around Paris.

"Until I get into the books and read through all that mumbo jumbo that the lawyer spit out so fast on the phone when he called me, the only thing I know is that she banked in Midcity and that she named me as executor with the understanding that we were all three to inherit equally," Becky said. "I've got all the books out of the safe in the back room and ready to take to the house when Jodi gets here."

"Can you believe that she's up and around already?" Lainie asked.

"She came through a while ago and picked up some minnows. She said the smell of breakfast woke her up," Becky answered. "Maybe you should cook every morning. That way, we'll get her internal clock reset."

"Or maybe if she doesn't have anyone to party with, she'll fall asleep earlier," Lainie said.

"Maybe so," Becky said.

The door opened, and the small store was suddenly packed with men wearing their lucky hats with hooks and lures all over them, rubber boots, and big smiles. The buzz of conversations about fish the size of half-grown Angus bulls and bets about who would catch the biggest catfish that day got louder and louder. Finally, Lainie rang up the last sale, the men headed for the river, and the noise died down.

"Know what I was thinking about when they were all talking at once?" Lainie asked.

Becky laughed out loud. "The only difference between men and boys is the price of their toys."

"Yep." Lainie laughed with her. "Granny Lizzie used to say that all the time. She was right, you know. I figured it out a month before my wedding.

Eli was more interested in his fancy car collection and his big house with a pool and tennis courts than he was in me. I was going to be a trophy wife, and I wanted more than that."

"We all heard that he was rich and that he was into import and export, but how did he earn all that money?" Becky asked.

"He's a trust-fund baby who works when he wants to and golfs when he wants to, or travels when his folks need him to go make deals," Lainie answered. "I was intrigued by all that fancy stuff at the first, but then he started bossing me around like I was one of his possessions. I thought I was too far into the wedding to back out, but at the last minute…" She shrugged.

"Granny Lizzie would have been proud of you," Becky said.

"I was thinking about her the whole time Jodi was fixing our hair, and I could hear her telling me that I was making a big mistake. Do you think that was crazy?" Lainie asked.

"Was what crazy?" Jodi toted a cooler into the store. "I caught two nice-sized bass and a small catfish. I cleaned them, and they're cut up ready for you to cook. Now tell me who's crazy?"

"I was talking about me being a runaway bride." Lainie went on to tell Jodi what she'd said, ending with, "So, what do you think? Do you hear her voice in your head?"

"Oh, yeah, even when I haven't been throwing back shots." Jodi grinned. "When your dad came up the aisle alone and announced that there wouldn't be a wedding, my face turned so red that I thought it would go up in flames. I've never been so embarrassed for all of us and for your folks, but then Granny Lizzie's voice popped into my head and told me that you had your reasons."

Becky held up her hand like a little kid in school who wanted to say something. "Me too, but I was too mad at you to listen to her that day. Derrick and I broke up two years ago because he couldn't keep his hands or his eyes off other women, and I couldn't trust him. I can't imagine having someone controlling me like you said Eli was doing with you." She lowered her hand and poured them all a fresh glass of sweet tea.

"Oh, it went beyond just him," Lainie admitted. "He even wanted me to let his mother tell me how to dress, how to wear my hair and what color nail polish and lipstick to wear. And they wanted me to bleach my dark hair out to platinum like his mother's."

"Sweet Lord!" Jodi gasped. "No amount of money in the whole world is worth putting up with that crap. No wonder you ran away, but holy smoke, girl, couldn't you have done it before the ceremony had started?"

"I kept thinking about all the money Daddy had spent. He and Mama had to put on a big show since the other side was so wealthy," Lainie said. "I was miserable on the day of the wedding. Everyone kept telling me it was bridal jitters, but I knew in my heart that I'd made a huge mistake."

"Why didn't you tell us?" Becky asked.

"What would you have done? Be honest," Lainie said.

"I would have told you it was wedding jitters because I was jealous that you were marrying into one of the richest families in the state, and because I wanted to be in your shoes." Becky stopped, took a breath, and then went on. "And because Eli is so damn good-looking, and he was hanging all over you at the rehearsal dinner. Derrick would have been scoping out the other women."

"Not me." Jodi shook her head. "I would have

crawled out that window with you. Only we wouldn't have gone to a cheap motel. We would have holed up in a motel right on the beach and spent every day laying out in the sun. No man is ever going to tame me. I'll be the old-maid cousin who spoils y'all's kids and teaches them to fish right here on the banks of the river."

Becky got tickled and snorted. "Yeah, right, as if any of us are going to find someone in Catfish. We'll all be old maids and running this—"

"Whoa!" Lainie threw up a hand to protest. "One of us has to have a daughter so there will be someone to leave this place to when we're gone. We don't have to decide today which one it will be, and we damn sure don't have to decide if we do or do not want a husband or father of our child to be involved past getting one of us pregnant, but we do have to have a daughter."

"Becky can do it," Jodi said. "Chris was lookin' at her like she was the only woman on earth when I came in to get a fishing rod and reel from the back room earlier today. Besides, she's got it together better than me or you, and she's the oldest, so her biological clock is ticking the loudest."

"Hey, now!" Becky protested. "Don't be making

decisions like that for me, and Chris was not looking at me like that. He's just lonely since his grand-dad died. Granny Lizzie was his friend, and now she's gone and…"

"Who are you trying to convince?" Lainie asked. "Us or yourself?"

"Hush!" Becky blushed. "We don't even know if Chris has a girlfriend or maybe even a fiancée, so don't go picking out wedding cakes for me."

"Don't get all huffy," Jodi teased. "Evidently, none of us is any good at picking out men, so maybe we'll just pool our money and adopt a daughter for us all to share."

"Now, that sounds like something we should look into," Lainie agreed.

Becky was still thinking about what Lainie had said that afternoon when she carried a tote bag full of books from the store to the house. She sat down at the kitchen table and spread them all out in front of her, starting with the bank statements that her grandmother kept in a red three-ring binder.

"Holy crap on a cracker!" she gasped when she saw the March 1 balance in two different savings accounts and the checking account. Her eyes got even bigger when she opened the blue binder to find the investment portfolio. "Why did you live like a pauper?" Becky muttered.

A letter fluttered out of the investment portfolio and floated to the floor. When she picked it up, Becky saw her own name on the front of the envelope, in her grandmother's distinctive handwriting.

With trembling hands Becky tore into it, then unfolded the lined paper to read:

My dearest granddaughters, if you are reading this then I've stepped over the great divide from this life to the next. I've addressed this to Becky, but it's for all of you. You three girls have been the joy of my life. I raised three sons by myself after your grandfather died, and not a one of them wanted to stick around this area and help me run the store. I can understand and accept that, and they've all made something of themselves and given me you girls, so there's no complaints.

After I got the boys raised and through college, I didn't need much. Money is just dirty paper with dead presidents' pictures on it anyway, and it can't buy happiness or peace, so it just accumulated. You girls divide it and do whatever you want with it. I hope that at least one of you will keep the bait shop open. That's important to me since you'll be the fourth generation of Cornell women to run the place.

Know that I love each and every one of you. I couldn't ask for better granddaughters, but Becky, you need to keep an eye on Lainie. She's about to marry the wrong man, and there will be a divorce in her future. She's way too much like me to put up with someone telling her what to do and when to do it for the rest of her life. Take care of each other and stand together in times of trouble. A three-cord rope is hard to break.

It was signed, *Granny Lizzie.*

Becky put her head in her hands and wept until there were no more tears. "Oh, Granny, I'm so sorry that I didn't spend more time with you."

Your fifteen minutes of wallowing around in sadness are over. Now get up, wash your face, and get on with life. She'd heard her grandmother say those words too often to count when she and her two cousins would have a spat.

Without even thinking about it, she pushed back her chair, stood up, and went to the bathroom, where she washed her face and brushed her blond hair up into a ponytail. She went from there to the kitchen, where she got a cold beer—Granny's favorite kind—from the refrigerator and carried it out to the porch.

"Hey, got another one of those?" Chris asked from the bottom porch step.

"You already done with your guide trip?" She was so glad to see him that she could have run down the stairs and hugged him. He was the one other person who could appreciate Granny Lizzie's letter to the girls.

"Yep, and I already cleaned up my boat. Don't have another trip on the books until Thursday," he said, "unless you want to go out after you get off work tomorrow."

"Beer is in the fridge. Come on up here and go get one," she said.

"Thanks." He took the steps two at a time, went into the house, and came back with a cold beer in his hands.

She had sat down on the top step of the porch and rested her bare feet on the second one. He eased down beside her and stretched his long legs out to the third step down.

"Have you been crying? Your eyes are red."

She nodded and swiped a hand across her wet cheeks. "I just read a letter that Granny Lizzie wrote to us girls. She left it in the book work from the store. So, yes, I've been crying, and I expect Lainie and Jodi will do the same when they read it. Tell me about her last days, Chris. Was she sick?"

"Oh, no, honey." He scooted over closer to her and draped an arm around her shoulders. "She worked all day, locked up the store, and dropped. Rosco and Orville had been doing some night fishing and were on their way to their trucks when they heard her fall. They rushed up there, called 911, and they sent an ambulance, but the doctor said she was gone before she hit the porch, said it was most likely a blood clot that went through her heart. Since she'd signed a paper saying she didn't want an autopsy or to be put on life support, they sent her to the crematorium."

"How did they know to do all that?" Becky asked.

"She kept an envelope in her purse that had who to call and what to do," he explained. "The hospital folks called her lawyer, and he took care of the rest.

She told me once that she didn't want them to call you girls until things were all done."

"That's because we would have insisted on a proper funeral, and she knew it." Becky welled up again.

Chris brought a white handkerchief out of his pocket and handed it to her. "She knew y'all very well, but she wanted things done her way."

Becky wiped her eyes and handed it back to him. "We've been talking among us today—without arguing, if you can believe that. Right now, we're all staying on in Catfish and keeping the store open."

"I didn't have a letter from Grandpa when he died, but I had more time with him since he was sick for about a month before he passed away," Chris said. "I was shocked out of my wits when I found out how much he'd socked away through the years. He paid me a decent salary. Enough that I could live and still build up a decent savings account. Money didn't mean much to him or to Miz Lizzie. She told me that she was leaving you girls enough so that you could be independent. That's kind of what Grandpa did for me."

"You ever think of leaving this area and doing something else?" Becky asked.

"Couple of times, but when I get in that mood, I drive over to Paris, and just being in a town that size takes away my peace," Chris said. "Besides, I like being a fishing guide. I have all the work I can handle, and most of the time people are happy when they're fishing. I don't imagine that I'll ever leave Catfish."

"I never asked, but do you live close by here?" She turned up her beer for another drink.

"About two miles due west of here, right up in the bend of the river, in a house up on stilts like this because the Red has been known to flood," he answered.

"Did you always live with your grandparents?" she asked.

Chris shook his head. "My granny died one summer, and my folks were both killed in a car wreck that fall. Grandpa took me in and raised me from then on. I was seven years old that winter. I rode the bus to school for an hour each way, and he was always waiting for me when I got off it. He took me with him on his fishing trips on the weekends and evenings, and I couldn't have asked for a better role model." Chris chuckled. "Until I learned to cook, we lived on whatever he could heat up in the microwave because he was a lousy cook...except for fried fish. He was an expert at that, so we ate a lot of fish."

He moved his arm and set his bottle on the porch. "Your turn. Is your mama a good cook?"

"Oh, no!" Becky giggled. "Mama couldn't boil water without burning down the house. Daddy says that she thinks the smoke alarm is the timer. He can grill a good steak and smoke a brisket, but for the most part, we have a housekeeper and cook. Or I should say that they do. I haven't lived with them since I went away to college."

"And you?" he asked.

"I'm a fair cook," she answered. "Nothing like Lainie. She's a trained chef, but Granny Lizzie probably already told you that."

"Yep, she did," Chris nodded. "But I could sit here and listen to you talk until midnight."

"That's not a very good pickup line," she said, giggling.

"I've never been much good at flirting," he said, "because I just say what I think. Most women run the other way. Speaking of that, I should be going. I've got to make it to the bank before they close this evening to put in a deposit. I used to take Miz

Lizzie's bank bag with me once a week. If you girls trust me, I can save you a trip into Midcity anytime I'm going."

"We trust you, Chris," Becky said, "and I'm not running anywhere."

"You didn't answer me about going fishing tomorrow evening." He took a long drink from the bottle.

"Are you dating someone?" she asked.

"Nope," he answered. "Haven't been in a serious relationship in three years. Are you?"

She shook her head. "I broke up with my boyfriend two years ago. I have seen him every workday since because we were both employed by the same company and part of the accounting team. It hasn't been easy, and I'm glad to be away from there."

"Still no answer," he said.

"Chris, are you asking me out on a date?" She turned at the same time he did, and their eyes locked.

"I guess I am," he said, "but it's not anything fancy, like a nice restaurant and a movie afterward. It's just a float down the river with some fishing poles and a picnic supper."

"Who's bringing the supper?" she asked.

"I asked you, so I'll take care of that." He grinned.

"Then my answer is yes. I'll be ready at two thirty," she said.

"I'll be here at that time, then. I've wanted to ask you out for more than a decade. I had a big crush on you when we were teenagers," he admitted.

"There's been lots of times between then and now," she said, and their eyes locked for a moment.

"Miz Lizzie kept me informed about all you girls. She was very worried about you and Lainie, especially. She said Lainie would end up with a divorce, and she was afraid you'd get back with that ex because y'all worked together," Chris said. "You only came at Christmas, and I hated to butt into your time here, so…" He let the sentence hang and frowned.

"Anyway," he said, "I'm glad you're not running. Be great visitin' with you. I'll be here at two thirty tomorrow to walk you across the yard and down to the river."

"I'll be ready," she said.

Chapter 4

THE SKIES WERE STILL GRAY WHEN JODI CLOSED
up shop and headed back to the house that evening.
Evidently the Angels had curled up for the night
because there were no cats on the porch, and none
followed her across the parking lot and the yard.
She'd barely made it to the top step when Lainie
threw open the door and motioned her into the
house. "Hurry up. Becky has something to show us,
and she won't say a word until you're here."

"I don't want to have to say it twice, and besides,
you are both going to cry. I can't let anyone shed
tears alone, and I'm not sure I've got enough left for
two weeping jags," Becky said.

"I'm too tired to cry tonight," Jodi said. "Keeping
store, dipping minnows and all that, is tougher
than fixing hair all evening. Can we put this off
until morning?"

"We *cannot*!" Lainie said. "I cook when I'm nervous, and I've made chocolate chip cookies, peanut

butter cookies, and a lemon meringue pie, so we're going to hear Becky out and do our sobbing, and then eat."

"You didn't tell me there was food." Jodi headed straight for the kitchen, but when she got to the dining area, she stopped in her tracks and pointed. "What's all that? Are those the books you were talking about earlier? If so, I'm glad you're the accountant and not me. It looks like a lot of work."

"It is," Becky said, "but before we get into that, sit down with me here and read this letter that Granny Lizzie left us. Read it out loud, and that way, Lainie can hear it. I'll make two copies of it tomorrow so you can each have one, and also copies of the will if you want one for your records."

Jodi took the letter from Becky's hands and made it to the third sentence before her voice broke. She handed it off to Lainie and said, "You finish it. I can hear her voice in every word."

Lainie took it with shaky hands and with a trembling voice managed to read the rest of it; then she laid it on the table, wrapped Jodi up in her arms, and they both sobbed. Becky rounded the table, bent down, and made it a three-way hug.

"Now you see why I didn't want to say anything

until you were both here. My heart broke, and I felt so, so guilty when I read that." Becky finally raised up and wiped her eyes on a paper napkin, then handed it to Lainie. "We were always too busy to drive two and a half hours to see her, and now she's gone and left us a business, a home, and enough money that we could live for years without working again."

Lainie dried her eyes and tossed the napkin in the trash can. "She knew I was making a mistake marrying Eli. I'm glad I was a runaway bride."

"What do we do with the money?" Jodi asked. "I would use my part to buy either or both of your shares in this place, but you've said you don't want to sell."

"I guess we leave it where it is until we decide, and if any of us ever decides to move away, we will divide it up at that time. Until then, we can take a salary out of the store each week for our own, and maybe at the end of the year, divide the profits. How does that sound?" Becky asked.

"It sounds good to me," Lainie answered. "That way, we don't have to dip into our individual savings, and what's in all that"—she waved her hand around to take in all the papers on the table—"can just be our nest egg and grow until we're ready for it."

"Yes." Jodi's chin quivered, and a fresh batch of tears rolled down her high cheekbones. "I don't deserve any of this. I almost begged off last Christmas because I had a hangover."

"Aren't you glad you didn't?" Lainie said. "Now, go on into the living room. I'll bring in the cookies and pie and a pitcher of sweet tea…"

"I'd rather have a shot of Jack Daniel's," Jodi sobbed. "My hands are shaking too bad to even hold a cookie."

Becky opened a cabinet door, took down the bottle and glasses, and poured three shots. "I think we could all use one." She carried them to the living room, handed one to each of her cousins, and then held hers up. "To Granny Lizzie. May we all learn to be just like her—to appreciate what we have, not depend on anyone, and love each other like she wanted us to. Like she said, a three-cord rope is hard to break."

"Amen," Jodi and Lainie chorused.

"And according to Granny Lizzie, it was a sin to throw back good bourbon like they did in the old westerns, so we'll sip this shot and enjoy each drop," Jodi said as she turned up her glass and let the first bit slide down her throat. "It warms from the lips to the stomach, and just so y'all know, I'm pretty sure that we will always love each other, but that doesn't mean we'll always agree on everything."

"But Lord help whoever tries to drive us apart, be it man, woman, or fish," Lainie said.

"Amen," Becky agreed. "And just so y'all know, I'm going fishing with Chris tomorrow, and it's a real date. I don't want any teasing about it and no lip. Understood?"

"Yes, ma'am." Jodi grinned. "I knew that guy had a thing for you when we were just teenagers. We'll expect a full report when you get home tomorrow night."

"Who says I'll be home when y'all go to bed?" Becky asked with a twinkle in her blue eyes.

Jodi polished off the rest of her bourbon. "I just hope the first baby is a girl. What do you think, Lainie? Shall we name her Elizabeth after Granny Lizzie?"

"We could call her Beth and raise her from the beginning to know that someday she will own all this property," Lainie teased.

"On that note, I'm going to clean off the table and go to bed. Y'all are both crazy," Becky said.

"Even crazy is right once in a while," Jodi told her.

Chris showed up at the store thirty minutes after Becky opened the next morning. One look at him and her mind started running in circles. Chris had blue eyes and Becky's were brown, so if fate or destiny or God ever saw fit to put them together, would their child have blue or brown eyes? Her hair was blond, and Granny Lizzie called Chris's dishwater blond—somewhere between a true blond and light brown—so what color hair would their children have? With an effort, she pushed the questions from her mind.

"What can I do to help out this morning?" Chris asked as he poured two mugs full of coffee and handed one to Becky.

Before she could answer, the door opened and half a dozen guys and three women pushed their way inside. The women headed for the food aisles, and the guys went straight for the shelves with hooks, lures, and every other item a fisherman needed.

"Good mornin', let us know if there's anything we can help you with," Becky called out from behind the counter.

"Got any idea where we might get a guide at this

late date?" one of the women asked. "We've never fished in this area before."

"We heard it was the best place in the world for catfish," the tallest of the six men said.

"I'm a fishing guide," Chris answered, "and it is pretty good for catfish. I've never taken out a crew as big as you have. I only have one boat."

"We've got two boats ready to put into the water," the lady said. "How many can you take with you?"

"Three is all I can take," Chris said, "and six hours is the maximum time I stay out, so we'd have to be back at the dock by noon."

"Great, you are hired," the lady told him. "We'll divide up the bunch of us so we have three to your boat, and you can lead the way."

"You didn't ask how much I charge," Chris said.

"I don't care about price," the guy said. "And noon is fine. Can we leave right now?"

So much for having help for a few hours, Becky thought.

"Sorry," Chris whispered for Becky's ears only.

"No worries." She smiled. "See you later."

"I'll have to get a few things ready, but it shouldn't take more than fifteen minutes. Becky, I'll need three boxes each of worms, stink bait, and six dozen minnows," he said.

"We brought our own handmade lures," the lady said.

"You can leave them in the tackle box. If you want to catch catfish, the bait has to be alive or else stink, and the smellier the better. My boat is *The Shameless Hooker*, and it's docked by the pier. By the time you get yours in the water, I should be there," he said.

"You're the guide," the lady said as she and her friends carried their supplies to the counter.

Becky rang up everything, put the items in a bag, and made change, thinking the whole time that they must be planning to eat more than fish. Chris went straight back to the minnow tank and scooped up what he needed.

"Sorry about not sticking around to help," he apologized again.

"Your job comes first. After all, you've got to feed me this evening, so you better make a lot of money," she teased.

"Are you saying that you eat a lot?" His blue eyes twinkled when he joked.

"Why do you think I'm still single? Most men

never ask me out again after they pay the bill for a first-date dinner," she shot back at him.

"Then I guess I'd better get out there and charge these folks triple since there's three boatloads of them." He grinned. "Put all this on my bill. I usually come in and pay on the first of every month. Is that still acceptable?"

"If it was good enough for Granny Lizzie, it works for me." She put his items in a brown paper bag and handed it to him.

He gave her a brief nod and held the door open for Rosco and Orville on his way out. They asked a dozen questions about the folks in their fancy boats, got themselves a cup of coffee, and headed down to the pier to see if they could figure out where these newcomers were from.

Business was steady but not overwhelming, right up until Lainie arrived in midmorning with Jodi right behind her. "You're not supposed to come in until afternoon," Becky reminded her.

"I don't have anything else to do, and we need to talk," Jodi said.

"About what? Are you thinking of taking your part of the inheritance and leaving?" Becky asked.

Lainie set a plate on the counter and started

straightening shelves. "That's leftover fish from last night's supper. I thought we could share it for lunch today."

"I'm not going anywhere," Jodi said, "at least not for long. That's what we need to talk about, though."

Becky picked up the fish and carried it back to the storage room, set it on the old chrome table that had been there her whole life and probably long before she was born, and sat down in one of the chairs. "Okay, shoot! What is it?"

"We each have an apartment with rent coming due in less than two weeks," Lainie said. "We were thinking that each of us could take two days to go take care of moving our things out, but what do we do with the accumulation? With what's already here, I don't have room for my fancy cooking equipment, and yet are we ready to give away Granny Lizzie's stuff?"

"We need to figure out what we want to bring of our own into the house. There's a women's shelter over in Paris that would probably take everything we don't want," Jodi said. "I just bought a new sofa that makes out into a bed, but I can't bear to think of getting rid of that old brown plaid one in Granny Lizzie's living room. I remember all of us curling up on it and watching kid movies like *Shark Tale* and *The Little Mermaid* with her after she closed up the shop. I thought it was wonderful because we were getting to stay up late."

"Or *Steel Magnolias* and *Fried Green Tomatoes* when we got older," Lainie said.

"It's our living room now, and rather than make rash decisions, why don't we each rent a storage place to keep our things until we make up our minds. I'm sure there's plenty of them available in Midcity," Becky suggested. "In time, replacing an item or two at a time wouldn't be so painful. As far as your cooking things, Lainie, I vote that you bring them along. I'm sure Granny Lizzie won't care if we get rid of her pots and pans. She seldom touched them anyway."

"I like that idea," Jodi said. "Then how about sometime next week, we each take a day or two to take care of those things. I can drive down in the morning and be back by midnight, so I'll only be gone a day."

"While we're talking, there is one more thing we need to think about. When we bring our clothing in, we need more closet room. Are we ready to pack up Granny Lizzie's things and donate them to that women's shelter?" Becky asked. "If so, maybe we could start that tonight. I'm already tired of living out of my suitcase."

"It won't be easy, but I think we should," Lainie agreed. "We've got plenty of boxes"—she waved her hand toward the empties at the back of the room—"and if we're not quite ready to give it all away, we can store the boxes in here."

"Now that we've made those decisions," Jodi said, "let's talk about something even more serious."

Becky couldn't think of anything that could top deciding to give up their apartments and pack away Granny Lizzie's clothing and other things. "And what would that be?"

"Chris and you," Lainie answered.

"That conversation is for another day. I hear footsteps on the porch. It's time for us to go to work," Becky said.

"Not me." Jodi headed out the back door. "I've got four hours until my shift begins. I'm going for a long walk beside the river. Save me a piece of fish."

"We'll think about it." Lainie headed to the front of the store to wait on the new customers.

Becky and Lainie were so busy that they ate their lunch on the run, taking bites between customers.

The holiday season around Thanksgiving and Christmas was hit or miss when it came to fishing, but spring—March and April in particular—were the big months in Catfish, Texas. More dust was stirred up on the dirt road in and out of the little community than any other time of the year.

"Hey, it's five after two. Don't you have a date this afternoon?" Lainie pointed at the clock after a couple of ladies had just checked out.

"Yes, I do, but Jodi…" Becky started to say, and then Jodi came through the door.

"Did I hear my name? I'm here. Go home and put on some lipstick, and take a shower to get the fish smell off of you. You've got a date with a sexy guy this afternoon." Jodi held the door open for her.

Becky jogged from the store to the house, left a trail of clothing from the living room to the bathroom, and took the fastest shower she'd ever had in her life. She dressed in denim shorts and a T-shirt, crammed her feet down into her oldest Nikes, and slung a lightweight jacket over her shoulder.

Chris was waiting on the top step when she went out onto the porch. She realized that even though she'd taken time to put her hair up in a ponytail, she hadn't even thought of makeup.

Too late now, she thought.

Chris held out a hand to help her down the steps. "You are beautiful, but that's no surprise. You've always been gorgeous." His eyes and the smile on his face said that he wasn't shooting her a line of crap.

"Thank you, but…"

He put a finger over her lips, sending delicious little tingles down her backbone. "There are no buts in the truth."

When they reached the ground, he kept her hand in his all the way past the store and down to the river where he helped her into his boat. "I know a nice peaceful cove where we can sit back in the shade and sweet-talk some fish into biting."

Becky took her seat beside him and looked around. Four seats, a canopy to shade his customers, a shiny black Mercury motor to get him anywhere on the river, and all the amenities for comfort. He started the engine and sat down beside her.

"Beer, sweet tea, or lemonade?" he asked.

"Cold lemonade would be great." She felt like a queen sitting on a throne instead of plain old Becky Cornell perched on a seat in a fishing boat.

He reached to his left, opened a container at the

side of *The Shameless Hooker*, and brought out two bottles of icy-cold lemonade.

She twisted the lid off her bottle and took a sip. "Why would your grandfather ever name his boat something like this?"

"To make a long story short, he bought this before my grandmother died and she said he should name it *Shameless Hooker* because most men stretch the truth when it comes to the size of the fish they catch." Chris chuckled. "He thought it was a hoot, so that's her name."

"It looks really good to be that old," Becky said, "but then I don't know jack squat about boats. Granny Lizzie and us three cousins fished right off the bank or maybe up on the pier."

"Grandpa and I kept the maintenance done on her." Chris patted the steering wheel. "They just don't build good quality now like they did when they made her. We had to buy a couple of new motors through the years, but this old girl still has a lot of wear in her."

"The way you fishermen talk about your boats like they're ladies, you should change her name to *Shameless Hussy*," Becky suggested.

"If I ever get another one, I just might do that."

Chris smiled as he steered the boat into a bend in the river that had willow trees growing right out into the shallow part of the deep-red water. "This looks like a good shady spot to drop anchor and fish a while."

"You're the famous guide around here, so I won't argue." She picked up a rod and reel and opened a box of worms.

"Want me to bait your hook?" he asked.

"I've been doing this since I was three years old." She laced the wiggly worm onto the hook. "Granny Lizzie said that if we were old enough to fish, we were old enough to bait our own hooks."

"A woman that baits her own hook"—Chris grinned and slid a sly wink her way—"is after my heart for sure."

Becky's ex, Derrick, had been very romantic— flowers, chocolates, sexy little notes in her desk drawer at work—but none of those things gave her the thrill that she got when Chris smiled and winked at her.

"What would I do with your heart?" she teased as she tossed her line over the side of the boat and watched the red-and-white bobber dance on the water.

"I'd hope that you would be nice to it and never

break it," Chris flirted as he baited his hook and dropped the line on the other side.

"Has it been broken before?" Becky asked.

"Cracked a couple of times, but not broken in half," he answered. "How about yours?"

"I thought it was shattered the first time my ex cheated on me, but looking back, I think it was probably just cracked. I got over it too quick for it to be a full-blown break," she admitted, "but if I talk about my ex, then you won't ask me out again, so let's change the subject."

"You'd go out with me again?" Chris gazed into her eyes.

"Yes, I would," she answered. "But you could be dating any woman in Texas. Why me?"

"Oh, come on." He chuckled. "How many women are truly interested in a guy who smells like fish and works the kind of hours I do? My granny could barely put up with Grandpa, and they don't make women like her anymore."

"You're comparing me to a grandmother? That's really romantic," Becky said.

"I'll make this simple." His eyes twinkled. "I've had a crush on you for more than a decade, and I don't care if women lined up at my door and begged me to go out with them. They still wouldn't interest me. I never thought I'd have the opportunity to date you and get to know you on a different level than just friends or acquaintances. I like you a lot, and I hope that I didn't just ruin things by saying all that."

"You did not." She leaned over and kissed him on the cheek. "You said just enough, and honey, your bobber just went under. I believe you've got a fish on the line."

"Any other time, I'd say that was good luck," he said as he began to reel in the fish, "but I'd rather have another kiss than a fish."

"Kisses don't feed us supper," she said, but she would have gladly given up food for a nice long make-out session.

You don't do that on a first date, the voice in her head scolded.

I would on this one, she argued. *I haven't had a date in two years, so I'm entitled.*

"I've got fried chicken in the cooler for supper." Chris reeled in a nice big alligator gar and quickly released it back into the river.

"Ever eaten one of those?" Becky asked.

"Yep." He rebaited his hook and tossed the line back out into the water. "Grandpa cooked them sometimes, but we were careful not to eat any of the eggs. They'll make you deathly sick. Now where were we on those kisses?" He grinned as he leaned toward her.

"Since we have supper in the cooler…" She moistened her lips with the tip of her tongue and felt a tug on her fishing rod at the same time. "I've got a bite."

"Bring it on in, and then we're going to the cove where I'd planned on getting out of the boat. I'm more interested in…" He chuckled when she brought up an old rubber boot.

"Guess between gars and boots, we aren't doing so good." She giggled.

"Oh, honey, I think we're doing just fine." He grinned as he unhooked the boot and tossed it back.

He put the rods away and drove to another bend in the river with a short pier. He set the cooler and a quilt up on the pier, hopped out, and secured the boat to a rail with a rope. Then he offered her a hand to help her up to the wooden platform.

Sparks danced around on the water like fireflies when she took his offered hand and let him pull her up onto the pier. "Where do we go from here?" she asked when she was steady on her feet.

"That's up to you." He flashed another grin,

this one even more brilliant than the last. "We can spread our quilt out right here, or we can take a little hike back on that pathway"—he pointed over his shoulder—"to a place up under a big willow tree, and pretend that we're in a five-star hotel."

"I'll carry the quilt." She picked it up and headed to the end of the eight-foot pier. "I like the idea of the Willow Bend Hotel."

"I never knew it to have a name." He picked up the cooler and followed her.

"Well, it does now, because when Jodi and Lainie ask me where we went, I want to tell them that we had a lovely meal at the Willow Bend Hotel." She walked down the four steps from the pier to the ground.

"Is it important to you that our date sounds fancy?" he asked.

"Nope," she answered. "I just want to tease them. In all reality, this is the most fun date I believe I've ever had."

"Oh, really? Surely you've been out at honest-to-God fancy restaurants. Right up ahead. See that weeping willow sitting out all by itself?"

"Sweet Lord!" she gasped and stopped in her tracks as she took in the sight of an enormous weeping willow tree with its limbs drooping all the way to the ground. Sunlight shining down in wide rays created an ethereal, surreal light around it as if it belonged in another world. "That is beautiful, Chris. Do many people know about this place?"

"Not that I know of. It's kind of been my secret since I discovered it five years ago," he answered. "I've been saving it just in case you ever said you'd go out with me."

She'd held her breath so long that her chest ached, and yet she was afraid if she sucked in more air or blinked, the whole beautiful scene would disappear. The sight, plus what he'd just said, was by far more romantic than anything anyone had ever shown her or said to her.

He walked a couple of steps ahead of her and said, "Follow me." He parted the limbs covered with soft green, minty leaves and stood to the side as if he'd opened the door for her. The small enclosure, with walls draped in curtains of leaves and the floor covered with green grass, smelled like fresh spring rain.

"This is amazing, Chris. There are no words." She entered the area and tossed out the quilt. "Have you really never..."

He set the cooler down. "Never." He finished the sentence for her. "If I couldn't share it with you, then I'd just keep it for myself. If you will take a seat, I'll get out a couple of beers."

Becky was speechless and scolded herself for not seeing what an amazing guy Chris was years and years ago. Talk, nothing! Becky wanted to hug him, really kiss him, and tell him how he had made her feel. She sat down in the middle of the quilt, and he brought out four candles in jars, lit them, and set them on all four corners of the quilt.

"Citronella." He eased down beside her. "There's nothing romantic about swatting mosquitoes all evening." He opened the cooler again, removed two longneck bottles of beer, and twisted the top off hers before he handed it to her.

"I thought about bringing champagne, but I would have been late to pick you up if I'd had to drive all the way to Midcity to get it," he said.

"I like beer better," she told him as she took a long sip. "It's so peaceful here that I could spend hours—no, days—right here."

"That's why I love it so much," he said, "and I'm so glad you feel the same way."

He took the bottle from her and set both his and

hers back in the cooler, tipped her chin up with his knuckles, and kissed her—long, lingering, and passionate. His hands moved to cup her face as that kiss led to another and then another. She was glad that she was sitting down because her knees felt as if they were too weak to support her. Her pulse raced, and her heart thumped in her chest like a drum. Derrick's kisses had never affected her like this, and his touch on her cheeks and that soft part of her neck right below her ear hadn't taken her breath away either.

When Chris finally broke away and handed her the bottle of beer, she said, "I've kissed on first dates, but sweet Lord." She gasped and took another long drink.

"It was even better than I'd dreamed it might be." He draped an arm around her shoulders and drew her closer to him.

She'd never thought about kissing Chris, much less dreamed about him, until she'd come back to Catfish, and now she wondered exactly why she hadn't.

Chapter 5

BECKY FELT LIKE A TEENAGER WHO HAD BEEN making out with her boyfriend when Chris walked her home from the river that evening. If she was glowing as much as he was, there was no way Lainie and Jodi would ever believe that they had only made out under the willow tree that evening.

"This has been the most amazing date I've ever had," she whispered as hand in hand they climbed the steps to the porch. "'Thank you' doesn't seem like enough to say."

"That you're going out with me again is thanks enough." He stopped at the door and dropped her hand. With several inches between them, he leaned forward and brushed a sweet kiss across her lips. "Good night, Becky. I'll see you in the morning."

"Good night, Chris," she said and watched him disappear down the steps and into the darkness.

She didn't want him to go, but there was no

way she would invite him inside. She wasn't ready to share him in any way with her two cousins, not even with conversation over a cup of coffee. What she'd like to do would be to walk right past them, take a quick shower, and crawl into bed and dream about Chris. But that wasn't about to happen. They would be sitting on the sofa, all bright-eyed and demanding details.

With a long sigh, she opened the door and entered the living room to find tissues scattered all over the floor, and Jodi and Lainie both sobbing. Becky glanced at the clock and was surprised to see that it was only ten fifteen. She'd lost track of time but figured it would be well past midnight.

Her euphoria vanished as she eased down on the sofa between them, fully expecting to hear that someone had died in the family and selfishly hoping that it wasn't her mother or father.

"Who is it?" Becky wiped at the tears beginning to flow down her cheeks. She never could let Lainie or Jodi cry alone, even if she thought they deserved to be weeping.

"Granny Lizzie." Jodi handed her the box of tissues that she'd been holding in her lap.

Becky pulled one out and wiped her face. "Why

are we having another crying jag now? Granny Lizzie's been gone for a couple of weeks."

Lainie pointed to a brown box on the coffee table. "The man from the crematorium delivered that this evening."

"It seems so wrong to think that's all that's left of her." Jodi pulled out two tissues and blew her nose loudly. "I can feel her spirit in this house and in the store. Those ashes can't be her. Seeing them sitting there makes things so final."

"Do you think that she won't ever pop into our thoughts again?" Lainie asked.

"I'm going to choose to believe that as long as we are alive and keep memories of her in our hearts, she will always be here to guide us and to give us advice. Just because we weren't right here in the house or the store with her after we were grown didn't mean that we didn't hear her voice in our heads, did it?" Becky wasn't sure if she was trying to convince Lainie and Jodi or herself.

"I knew that she was with me when I ran out on my wedding," Lainie said.

"And we all three had no doubts that she wanted us to keep the store and this place going when she died," Jodi answered.

"Then we'll do what she wants with those"—Becky's voice cracked when she pointed at the simple cardboard box—"and scatter them in the Red River like she asked. Let's close up shop at five on Sunday evening and do it then. I've asked Chris to join us, and I'm sure he won't mind taking the three of us out in his boat so we can make sure that Granny Lizzie is floating down the river to where Grandpa is. That's what she asked for in her will."

"This Sunday?" Lainie frowned. "I'm not sure I'll be ready to let go of even that"—she stared at the box of ashes—"so soon."

"We'll be sad until it's done"—Jodi agreed with Becky—"so let's just do it on Sunday and let her go be with Grandpa. That's what she'd want, whether we're ready or not."

"You're right," Lainie said, "and it's the guilt talking because we didn't come back to see her nearly often enough."

"All right then, Sunday it is," Becky said. "I vote we leave her right there until then and that we each remember something about her or something she said until we take her out in the middle of the river. On that note, I'm going to bed. I'm the one who has to get up early tomorrow."

"Oh, no!" Lainie wiped her eyes one more time. "Not until you tell us what happened on the date. We need to hear something good, and besides, Granny Lizzie wants to know the details about you and Chris before she goes to see Grandpa. She's always loved that guy, and she's very excited that you went on a date with him."

"How do you know that?" Becky yawned.

"She told me," Lainie answered.

"I'll tell you tomorrow." Becky started to stand up. Jodi got her by the arm and pulled her back down. "I'll get up early and take your shift if you want to sleep in, but we've cried for hours, and we need to hear something positive."

"What if"—Becky yawned again—"it's not positive?"

"Has to be," Lainie said. "You were glowing when you walked into the house. Where did you go? Did he kiss you?"

"Did you catch any fish? Did the kiss make your toes tingle?" Jodi asked.

"I caught an old rubber boot, and Chris caught a gar. We threw them both back," Becky answered. "He kissed me more than once, and we spent the evening under an amazing weeping willow tree.

And yes, the kisses made my toes tingle. I've never had sex on a first date, but I dang sure thought about it tonight. Anything else?"

"We wouldn't have judged you if you'd brought him in for the night," Lainie said.

"Shhh…" Jodi giggled and pointed to the box. "Granny Lizzie really loved Chris, but I wouldn't have the nerve to have sex in her room with her sitting in the living room, and I'm the most brazen one of the three of us."

"Did you run away minutes before your wedding?" Lainie challenged her. "I think that makes me even sassier than you."

Becky stood up and waved over her shoulder. "I'll let both of you fight for the crown. I'm going to bed, and"—she turned around—"I hope I dream of Chris, because even after just one date, I can see a future with him."

"Good night," Lainie said. "If we hear you moaning, we'll know it's a really good dream."

Becky tried to fight off the blush, but it was impossible. Living with those two as adults was sure different than it had been when they were just kids.

Chapter 6

ON SUNDAY MORNING BECKY AWOKE TO RAIN beating against her bedroom window. She grabbed the extra pillow and crammed it down on her head. "I shouldn't have stayed out until past midnight with Chris," she muttered.

Was it worth it? Granny Lizzie's voice was clear in her head.

Becky tossed the pillow on the foot of the bed and sat up. "Yep, it was, and I'll do it again, I'm sure," she said as she slung her legs out over the side of the bed and stood up.

She got dressed, pulled her hair up into a ponytail, and started to put on a pair of athletic shoes, but then she noticed Granny Lizzie's cowboy boots in the closet. She shoved her shoes into a tote bag and slipped her feet into the boots. They were a perfect fit, and hopefully would keep her feet from getting wet. She searched everywhere for an umbrella, but couldn't find one, so she went back to the bedroom and pulled out an old yellow slicker.

When she opened the door, Chris was standing on the porch, also wearing a yellow slicker and a smile. "Thought you might need a Prince Charming to come rescue you this morning."

"Thank you! This maiden in distress appreciates your sweet kindness. If this doesn't stop, the river is going to be too high and wild to go out this afternoon." She closed the door behind her.

He draped an arm around her shoulders and held an umbrella over them. "It's supposed to clear off at noon, and the sun is supposed to come out bright. That means high humidity, but it shouldn't keep us from our memorial for Miz Lizzie. I've made a little supper for us afterward," he said as they started up the steps to the store. "It's just soup and finger foods, but I thought it would be nice to have something at my house for her. I hope I'm not overstepping my boundaries."

"There are no boundaries or fences between good friends." Becky opened the door and flipped on the lights. "Surely you don't have a job this morning."

He closed the umbrella, set it against the counter, and helped her remove her slicker, and then took his off and hung them both on a coatrack just inside the door. Then he gathered her up in his arms and hugged her tightly. "I should be sad about this afternoon, but every time I think of Miz Lizzie, she's smiling because we're dating."

"Me too. I think this would make her very happy," Becky said.

Chris tipped up her chin to kiss her, but before his lips touched hers, the door swung open and the wind seemed to blow Jodi and Lainie both into the store.

"Don't let us interrupt you." Jodi grinned.

"What are y'all doing here?" Becky asked.

"The power went out in the house. That means the air conditioner doesn't work, and we can't make coffee, so we threw some clothes in a tote bag." Lainie held up one of those lined bags meant to keep things hot or cold.

"We're soaked so we're going to the back room to change into dry things, so you two carry on," Jodi teased as she headed across the room. "Don't let us interfere with your make-out session."

Lainie gave them a broad wink. "We'll take our time changing."

Becky wrapped her arms around Chris's neck

and said, "We may need the room when y'all are done with it."

Jodi stopped in her tracks. "Granny Lizzie would haunt you."

Becky giggled. "Gotcha! Don't dish out the joking if you can't take it in."

"Who's joking?" Chris chuckled.

"Dammit!" Lainie grabbed a paper towel from the coffee area and wiped her eyes. "Just thinking about Granny Lizzie makes me emotional." She looked down at Becky's feet. "Aren't those Granny Lizzie's boots? How come you get to wear them?"

"Because you and Jodi have feet that won't fit into them," she answered.

"Do y'all think we'll be able to have her memorial this afternoon in all this rain?" Jodi asked.

"I've ordered sunshine after lunch." Chris kissed Becky on the forehead. "We'll have the coffee ready when y'all are done changing."

"And honey buns right off the shelf." Becky grinned.

"At least we've got electricity so we can see to eat them." Jodi closed the door behind her and Lainie.

"Now, where were we?" Chris drew Becky to his

chest for a long, steamy kiss, and then he set about making a pot of coffee.

Becky took a dozen honey buns from the rack, removed the wrappers from four, and put them on paper plates. "Want yours cold or hot?"

Chris chuckled. "I like my honey buns cold, but I like my honey hot. Which one are we talking about?"

Becky air slapped him on the arm. "You are funny, Chris Adams. Why didn't you ever show me your sense of humor when we were kids?"

"Because I was so tongue-tied that I couldn't even say a word to you," he admitted.

"Well, thank goodness we're grown up now because I love your sense of humor," Becky said.

"Thank you. I kind of like yours too." He carried two of the plates to the counter at the front of the store.

———

For once, the weatherman was right. The clouds shifted on across the Red River into Oklahoma at noon, and by five o'clock that afternoon, the sun was shining brightly as it made its way to the western horizon. Chris helped each of the women into his boat and got them settled into the seats.

The trip out to the middle of the Red River took only a few minutes, but it seemed like forever. Becky held the box of ashes on her lap and dreaded what was to come next. She wasn't sure that she could let the gray dust sift through her fingers into the water.

It's what I want. Granny Lizzie's voice in her head was stern.

"I'm not sure I can do this," Lainie said. "This whole week has been so emotional. I know today is not about me, but my heart feels like it's got a stone tied around it."

"Granny just now told me that this is what she wants," Becky said.

"All right." Chris killed the engine and reached for the box. "I've added a little bit to this ceremony. I hope you girls don't mind." He laid his phone down and touched the screen. Chris Stapleton's voice singing "Broken Halos" floated out down the river.

He opened the box, and Lainie stepped up to dip her hand into the ashes as the lyrics said that he'd seen his share of broken halos that used to shine. With tears in her eyes, she let the gray ash filter through her fingers, and then she sat back down.

Jodi took the next turn as Stapleton said that we shouldn't go looking for the answers or asking Jesus why because we weren't meant to know the answers. She held her head high as she did the same thing that Lainie had done and watched through tears as her fistful of ashes lay on top of the water for a few minutes before the water took them downstream.

Chris set the box on his seat, and together he and Becky took out a handful to the words that talked about folded wings that used to fly. He held her free hand in his, and they tossed their part of the ashes out onto the water.

Then Becky picked up the plastic bag holding the rest of Granny Lizzie and dumped it all at once into the water. Chris took a couple of tissues from a box that he pulled out from under his seat, and then handed it to Becky. She pulled out one and passed the box to Lainie and Jodi.

The song ended, and they all sat watching the ashes float down the river for several minutes.

"Thank you, Chris," Lainie said. "That was so fitting and so special."

"I'll think of Granny every time I hear that song now," Jodi said.

Becky swallowed hard. "This isn't the end." She looked right into Chris's eyes. "This is just the beginning for all of us, and Granny Lizzie would like that."

The Third Wish

Wish

Carolyn Brown

Chapter 1

MY SISTER, ASHLEY, WAS EIGHTEEN THE SUMMER that our mother took us to the beach in Pensacola, Florida. The trip was Ashley's high school graduation present and birthday present rolled into one. I can still close my eyes and smell the salty air, and if I wiggle my toes, I can imagine that I'm playing in the warm sand.

And we got to stay for a whole week. We swam, collected shells, fed the gulls, and every night we watched the sun set over the water. I was eight that year, and to me the whole time was dusted with miraculous fairy dust.

We had a picnic on the beach on Ashley's birthday. Just the three of us—Mama, Ashley, and me—but there was pizza and a chocolate cake with candles. That was the second day of our weeklong trip. By then, I had fallen in love with the beach and made myself a promise that I would come back as often as I could.

Ashley and I found the old bottle washed up on the beach the night of her birthday. It was most likely a tequila bottle, but I was convinced that it was magic and that if we rubbed it hard, a genie would come out the top in a puff of smoke and grant us each three wishes. I shut my eyes and rubbed the bottle.

"Oh. My. Goodness!" Mama squealed.

My eyes popped wide open, but all I saw was a sunset reflected in the water. "What is it, Mama?"

"I saw the genie. He smiled at me and waved as he headed for the snow-cone shop down the strip."

I glanced over at Ashley. She was my idol, and more than once I wished that I was like her and Mama—petite, gorgeous brunette, graceful—but I was tall, blond, brown-eyed and clumsy.

"I saw him, too." She nodded. "And we each get three wishes."

Ashley wished for college to be easy, for no rain the rest of our vacation, and for a handsome prince to come into her life and sweep her away to live happily ever after. It took a few years but her wishes all came true.

Mama asked that her daughters, Ashley and Jessica—that would be me—would find happiness;

that she would live long enough to see her grand-children, and for the three of us to always respect and love each other. Her wishes also came true. Ashley and I were both happy. Mama got to see two grandchildren and watch them grow up to be fine young men, and we really did all three love each other.

I rubbed the bottle a few extra times because I wanted to really see the genie pop back in the bottle so I could take him home with me, but he wouldn't show himself a second time. So, I made my choices: the first was that I would find a big, huge conch shell the next day. And the second wish was that I could see my father. The third was that someday I'd fall in love and live happily ever after like the princess in the *Cinderella* movie. I did find a conch shell the next day. It wasn't big but it still sits on a shelf, along with the bottle, in my living room to remind me of the good times we had that summer.

That was twenty years ago, and my second and third wishes still hadn't come true. Then on a Thursday afternoon, a deputy sheriff came to our real estate agency with the news that our mother had been killed in a car wreck south of Jefferson,

Texas, where we live. A semi driver had lost control and slammed into her little smart car that she whipped around town in. She and the driver were both gone before the ambulance arrived on the scene.

The consensus in Jefferson, Texas, has always been that everyone knows everyone, knows what they are doing, and who they are doing it with, and they read the weekly paper to see who got caught. We knew Thomas, the deputy, and the way that tears ran down his eyes, I wondered if maybe he was my father. But even in my immediate and overwhelming grief, I knew that couldn't be true. The whole town would have known, and that bit of gossip was too juicy not to spread like a Texas wildfire.

Of all the things other kids had when I was a little girl, the thing I envied the most was that they had a father. Some of them even had two—a real daddy and a stepfather. It didn't seem fair to me that they got two, and I didn't have even one. Eventually, I realized that having a mother like I did made up for no father. Maybe that's why I was in denial so long after she was killed. I had lost both mother and father that evening when Thomas brought the news to us. Six weeks later, I was still in denial and refusing to take the next step—as Ashley called it—in the grieving process.

"Tomorrow morning, we are going through Mama's things and putting the house on the market," Ashley said.

"No!" I wailed and tears began to roll down my cheeks. "We can't touch a thing in our childhood home. That holds all our memories."

"Our memories are in our hearts." Ashley hugged me until I got the weeping under control. "And Mama wouldn't want a shrine. She would want us to move on and live our lives. All this sadness robs us of happiness."

"I can't do it," I declared. "You'll have to take care of it, Sister. I can't get rid of her things, and I can't move on."

"Yes! You! Can!" Ashley took me by the shoulders and looked right into my eyes. "And. You. Will."

"Can we just wait another month?" I begged.

"No, we are doing it tomorrow." She didn't leave any room for argument, so the next morning at eight o'clock, we met at Mama's house. My shoes felt like they were filled with concrete, making my feet so heavy as I walked from the car to the porch.

We had lived in this house my whole life, and most of Ashley's. How could we just treat it like any other place on the listing at our real estate office?

"Here's what I've got in mind," Ashley said. "We are going to go through her personal things and take what we want. If there's anything, furniture-wise, that either of us wants to keep, we will mark it, and when the women's shelter people come to take it all away, they will leave those pieces."

"Women's shelter?" I frowned.

"I made the decision to give what we don't want to the shelter in Tyler. Mama was all for empowering women, so I think she would like that idea." Ashley handed me a roll of masking tape. "Put a strip on anything you want and sign your name. Be sure it's visible."

"I want to keep it all," I told her. "Can't we just rent a storage unit and…"

She didn't give me time to finish but butted in. "And let it all get gnawed by rats and ruined by heat and cold? Mama would want it to go to a good cause. We'll start in her bedroom. I'll go through the dresser drawers, and you can clean out the closet. Do you want to keep her bed?"

She took me by the hand as if I were still eight

years old and led me down the short hallway to the bedroom. I couldn't remember how many nights I'd gotten in bed with Mama when I was a little girl. I was terrified of storms, and never—not once—had Mama scolded me.

Let me go in peace, Mama's voice was so clear in my head that I turned around to see if she was in the room with me. *I love you, Jess, but you've got to let me go.*

"I don't want the bed," I muttered.

"Okay, then," Ashley swiped away a tear. "Anything that you can't bear to part with out of the closet, just throw on the bed. I'm sure the women's shelter will be glad to take any of her clothing or shoes that we don't want to keep. I want the dress she wore to my wedding, so put it to one side."

By midmorning the closet was empty. I had kept the tears at bay until I found the T-shirt she had worn when we made the trip to Florida almost twenty years ago. I would decide later what to do with it, but I had to keep it.

I started on the shelves of shoes next. Mama had even smaller feet than Ashley, and I wear a size nine, so neither of us sisters wanted to keep any of those. I set them all on the other side of the bed for the women's shelter. I was taking them down three boxes at a time, and on the last trip, the top one tumbled off, and letters spilled out on the floor. Some of them were tied up with a faded red ribbon. The return address said they were from some guy named Edward Rollin. I'd never heard her mention the man, and I was intrigued.

"You leave those alone," Ashley said. "If that's who I think it is, she wouldn't want us to read them."

"Who do you think it is?" I turned them over several times in my hands. "And why would he write letters to Mama? I realize it was almost thirty years ago, according to the postmarks, but they did have phones."

"She went out with a guy when I was a little girl," Ashley said. "His name was Eddie, and she cried when they broke up. Those are private, and we need to burn them. If she'd wanted us to read them, she would have said so in her will. And girl, we had a phone, but we didn't have email, Snapchat, FaceTime, or smartphones like we have today. People still wrote letters back then."

"I'm reading them." I untied the ribbon and laid it aside.

Ashley stormed off to clean out more dresser

drawers. I figured that she was getting into things even more personal than I was. I took the letters to the living room, sat down in the middle of the floor, sorted them according to the dates on the outside, and began to read.

Three hours later, with big drops of tears still dripping from my cheekbones, I had read every one of them at least once and the last one that had never been mailed three times. My head hurt from sobbing and my eyes were bloodred. My father was Edward Rollin and he'd written half the letters I'd read; the other half Mama had sent to him. They wrote about very personal things, leaving no doubt that they'd had a hot and heavy romance for a few months.

Ashley had long since forsaken me and gone home so I sat there alone in Mama's bedroom and felt the pain she must've felt when she'd gotten the last letter from him. I found it in the box along with all the ones that she had written to him. He had sent all her letters back to her, but she must have loved him too much to give his back.

No wonder she'd always evaded my questions about my father. He'd thrown her away for another woman, and there was a possibility I had a half sister or brother somewhere in the panhandle of Florida. I could understand why she refused to tell me anything. I would have begged her to take me to meet my sister or brother. I would have cried to see my father. It was easier to say nothing than it would have been to deal with my whining.

It was late that Friday night when I dried my eyes and made my decision. I was leaving on Monday morning to go see Edward Rollin. I might not ever speak to him, but I was going to lay eyes on the man who broke my mama's heart and who fathered me.

Two days later, on the third Monday morning in August, I was packed to go to Panama City Beach, Florida, with all those letters tucked into the pocket of one of my suitcases. Ashley, in her usual bossy mode, was standing between me and the front door of my small house. Her arms were crossed over her chest. Her blue eyes flashed anger, and her delicate little mouth was set in a firm line.

"You are batshit crazy," she said through clenched teeth. "It's been more than twenty-eight years. He may have moved. He may be dead. Maybe he just told Mama that about another woman and child to break up with her. I can tell you right now he won't greet you with open arms and a big, happy welcome. Think, Sister! For God's sake, use that big, beautiful brain that you got from Mama and think about what you are doing. Mama had to have been thinking about the effect meeting him would have on you when she protected you from ever knowing him."

"I'm not stupid." I tossed two bikinis into the suitcase, planning to spend lots of hours on the beach even if I didn't get to meet or see my father. "I don't expect anything, so I won't be disappointed. Don't worry about me and my big, beautiful brain. I can take care of myself and my brain as well. Do you know what I always envied in other children? Everyone had a father but me—even you. Granted your daddy was dead, but at least you had one. I never even knew my father's name or what he did or where he lived. I didn't know if he was a bum or a millionaire."

"What makes you think seeing this man will bring you closure?" Ashley asked. "You're not a little kid who doesn't have a daddy at the father-daughter Valentine's dance at school. I didn't have one either and I survived."

"Nothing you can say will keep me from going, and when I get back, I promise it'll be finished." I zipped the suitcase and crossed the room with my usual long strides to bend down and hug my sister. I tower over my short sister and usually tease her about it being a sacrifice to bend so far to hug her, but not that day. There was nothing funny about our argument or the hug.

If our birth certificates didn't say that we had the same mother, even we wouldn't believe that we are sisters. She's a short, dark-haired, blue-eyed brunette just like Mama was. I'm a tall blonde with brown eyes. She's the bossy one. I'm the nosy one. The only thing that we really had in common was our mother, Linda. Well, that and the real estate agency that our family had run for more than forty years.

"Why don't you take a few days and go out to the farm? Think about it instead of going off in a tizzy like this. The farmhouse is so peaceful, and you like it there," Ashley pleaded.

"You can't talk me out of this," I told her. "Take care of my cat. Don't forget to water the ferns and give Callie a lot of attention while I'm gone, but don't give her the cat treats but once a day." I needed to see for myself the man who fathered me, not just read about how much my mama loved him.

Sure, he was probably married. The last letter he sent along with all the other ones that she'd mailed to him said that his girlfriend of seven years was pregnant, and he was going to do the right thing and marry her.

"Promise me you won't come dragging a broken heart back here." Ashley wasn't going to give up easily.

"I promise." I hugged her one more time. "I'll call when I check into the motel. I want to be so close to the water that I can smell the salt in the air. Remember when we would take deep breaths just to inhale the smell of salt water? See you in a couple of weeks. And keep the special cat treats out of sight, or Callie will meow until you want to wring her pretty calico neck."

The sun was a sliver in the east when I left Jefferson that morning. I listened to the old country songs that Mama loved the whole time it took me to reach the Sugar Sands hotel just east of Panama City Beach. I checked in, unloaded my stuff into my room, and stepped out onto the deck that led straight to the beach. In a couple of hours, it would be dark, and I wanted to see the sunset. Already, a brilliant array of colors reflected from the water as the sun got lower in the sky. To me, it seemed like an omen that I had seen a Texas sunrise and would shortly see a Florida sunset on the same day. Could it possibly be that one of the wishes I'd made on the washed-up bottle twenty years ago right there on a beach just down the coast from where we had been would come true?

Lazy waves lapped up on the sand and then retreated. Birds pecked through the sand and then rushed away from the water as it returned. The salty smell and the sound took me back to the last time I'd been in Florida. Even if I didn't find my father or my prince, maybe I'd find another bottle and make three more wishes.

What would you wish for? My mother's voice was back in my head.

"That I could go back in time and not even take the listing that you went out to show that day you were killed," I whispered. "That you would have told me about Edward, and that Ashley could realize how much it means to me just to see him in person if he's still alive."

I was leaning on the railing when the ringtone on my phone said that James, my best friend since kindergarten, was calling. I hit the button to answer but before I could say a word, he started on a world-class rant.

"Where are you? I've been worried all day. Why weren't you answering your phone calls? Ashley told me about this fool stunt. Why didn't you tell me? I'll tell you why. You didn't want me to talk you out of it," he rattled on.

I tried to get a word in edgewise, but about the time I opened my mouth, he had gotten a second wind.

"This is the craziest thing you've ever pulled. If your father wanted to see you, he'd have found you. You're giving up your whole vacation to chase an elusive dream. You don't act like this, Jessie. You've always had a good head on your shoulders, and you're too young to be going through a midlife crisis. You just flat out aren't the kind of woman who goes off chasing butterflies." He finally ran out of air.

I latched onto the chance to talk and said, "I'm here and it's just like I remembered only better, and the sun is setting, and you'd love it. You should catch a plane and fly down for two weeks. I didn't answer your calls because I didn't want to listen to you have a hissy like you just did," I told him, expecting another tirade about how foolish I was.

"I'm too mad to talk to you, so I'm hanging up before we both say things that we'll be sorry for." He was gone without so much as a goodbye.

I stomped into the room, picked up a pillow, and threw it at the wall. I wanted to scream loud enough that he could hear me all the way to Texas, but that wouldn't do a bit of good. So, I bit back tears of anger and frustration and changed into a bikini. Muttering about how that I'd prove him wrong, I threw a T-shirt over the top and tucked the room key card into my tote bag.

It was too late for suntanning, but I could at least feel the sand on my toes. I spread out my tie-dyed beach towel on the sand and lay back to enjoy the sound of the waves splashing up on the shore. I kept an eye out for another bottle that might wash up, but I guess the ocean was all out of empty tequila bottles that day.

At first, I had my knees pulled up under my chin, but then I wanted to feel the surf on my toes. Just as I stretched out my long legs, a jogger tripped over them and went flying out into the edge of the water face-first. He came up sputtering with fire in his blue eyes and his black hair dripping water onto his muscular body.

"Why did you trip me? Are you crazy? My MP3 player is ruined." His chest was broad, and muscles rippled under his tight, white tank top. My first thought was that he could probably win a wet T-shirt contest for men, and that the women would make him rich throwing dollar bills at him. My second was that his blue eyes could cut steel. My heart did a little quiver, like maybe it was telling me to be careful, but I ignored it. I never did like a smart-ass attitude, and I wasn't in the mood to play nice.

"Why don't you open your eyes and take those things out of your ears. Enjoy the sound of the ocean instead of listening to loud music. Maybe then you wouldn't nearly break a woman's leg with your big feet." I shot back.

Tomorrow, I'd have a bruise on my shin bone where his big foot slammed against it. Thank goodness he was barefoot, or he could have cracked the bone.

He glared at me for a moment, his jaw working like he was about to spit out a whole string of blistering-hot cuss words, but finally he set his mouth in a firm line and took off in a semi-jog, his wet clothing sticking to him and his bare feet slapping against the hard sand. He didn't look back once, and I watched him until he was nothing but a tiny moving dot against the setting sun. Then I got up and walked back toward to my room. It had everything I needed for a two-week visit—queen-size bed, small stove, refrigerator, big-screen television, sofa, table and four chairs, free Wi-Fi, and my own personal space on the deck.

The cool air hit me like a blast from the North Pole when I opened the door, and goose bumps popped up on my body. I turned down the air, went to the bathroom, and adjusted the water in the shower. That's when I remembered I was supposed to call Ashley.

I knew that she'd yell at me, so I set the phone on the table, pulled up a chair, and pushed the speaker button. She answered just like James had done earlier—with a tirade. "James called and said you were already there, and I tried ten times to call you and you didn't pick up. I was about to send out the troops. It's a cryin' shame when your friend gets to talk to you before I do, and I was beginning to worry really bad. Honest to God, you have no business doin' this and…" She stopped for a breath.

I had to jump in there and start talking fast

before she got her second wind. "I left my phone in the room and enjoyed the beach until some jogger tripped over my leg and fell into the water. He was pretty angry, but he should have been watching where he was going."

"I'm still mad, and that's no excuse. Keep your phone with you all the time. What if he'd been a serial killer and you couldn't even dial 911? What if he'd broken your leg and you couldn't get help and had to lie there in the sand until the tide washed you out in the ocean?"

"You're just jealous because I'm here and remembering all the good times we had that summer. You know what I did while I was on the beach? I looked for a bottle at the edge of the water, but I couldn't find one. I can take care of myself, but I'd sure like to spend time with you on this beach again before we're both too old to even enjoy it."

"You really think this agency can run itself for two whole weeks? Get real," she fussed. "We have to take separate vacations, or we won't have jobs to come back to."

I carried my toiletry kit into the bathroom and set it on the vanity. "You or Momma either one couldn't close the business for more than a day at a time, and as far as I'm concerned, folks could wait one week to close on a deal or look at a house."

"My sister and co-owner of the business is full of crap to think like that." Ashley's tone turned chilly. "Have you been to see him yet?"

"No, I'm waiting until morning. I wanted a little thinking time first. After that long drive, I'm pretty exhausted. I'm in Room 101, and there's a chair and a bench right outside my door on the deck. Tomorrow morning I'm going to drive downtown and look at the building where his mortgage company is located. According to the yellow pages, it's Rollin, Smith, and Rycroft. Sounds like three stuffy, old men who smoke cigars and sit in a big conference room deciding who gets a fancy loan and who doesn't. Is my cat missing me?"

"That rotten Callie doesn't even know you're gone. She got out of the carrier and claimed the piano stool in front of the bay window as her property. Trey feeds her a morsel at a time out of the palm of his hands," Ashley said.

"Trey's a good kid. Always trust a fellow who knows how to treat a cat," I told her. "I'll call tomorrow evening and let you know how it went."

"Don't hang up," Ashley said hurriedly. "I saw

James at Dairy Queen. He was grabbing a salad for lunch. He's still pretty mad at you. Said he was going to dinner tonight with one of the secretaries at the courthouse. What is her name? She's the one with short, dark hair and wears glasses."

"Colleen?" I hugged myself. For the past few months James had this crazy notion that he and I might be more than friends—an idea that I didn't share. So, I was glad to hear that, even in a fit of anger, he was trying to get past the idea of us settling into a comfortable permanent relationship. When and if I ever did take the plunge, it would be with all the bells and whistles and fireworks. I didn't see any of that happening if I got serious with James. He was laid-back, predictable, and I'd feel like I was dating my brother if I went out with him.

"Colleen? That's her name. Are you jealous?" Ashley asked.

"Not in the least. Maybe he'll fall so much in love with her in two weeks that he'll be lookin' at engagement rings when I get home. Give my love to Danny and the boys and kiss Callie for me."

"I don't kiss cats. I'll tell Trey to do it. Good night, Jessie."

"Good night," I said, and ended the call.

I had been ten years old when Ashley married Danny and was so proud to be a bridesmaid in her wedding. When they had their sons, barely two years apart, I had babysat for them. Now Graham was fourteen and would be in high school in three weeks and Trey was in the seventh grade. Ashley, her husband, Danny, and their sons, Graham and Trey—that was my family, all of it since Mama was gone. I loved every single one of them, but there was an unsatisfied ache in my soul that needed to see my father, even if he didn't know I existed.

Ashley hadn't known her father either, but Mama talked about him, and there were pictures taken on their wedding day. He'd worn his army uniform, and she'd worn a lace dress with bell sleeves and a white rose circlet in her hair.

When I'd asked about my father and wanted to see pictures of him, Mama had said that he was a guy she'd known for a short while who didn't stick around.

I heard the water running in the shower and remembered what I'd been doing when the phone rang. I dropped my clothing on the floor and stepped inside, letting the warmth beat some of the kinks from my back and neck. Then I flipped a fluffy, white towel around my long hair and one around my body. My hair was still damp when I pulled it up into a ponytail and slipped into my favorite faded nightshirt. That's when the jitters hit.

I headed straight for the goodie bag—as I called it—and opened a package of chocolate chip cookies. When I'm nervous, angry, or happy, I turn to food. Right then I was all three because I was going to see my father the next day.

Chapter 2

THE NEXT MORNING, I NERVOUSLY MADE MY WAY through the huge, crowded lobby to the information desk of the firm where supposedly my father was a partner. I had prepared a dozen speeches, but they'd all flown out of my mind like a butterfly flitting away to a flower a mile away.

The receptionist looked up at me. "May I help you?"

"I'm here to see..." I stammered. Did I call him Eddie like he signed his letters? I started all over. "I'm here to see Mr. Edward Rollin," I said with more bravado than I felt.

She motioned toward the elevator doors to the right of her desk. "It's about time. You're at least five minutes late. The mortgage firm is on the third floor, first door on the right. He's already called down here three times, so don't waste time."

"What?" I asked, wondering if my sister had called him that morning and told him I was arriving.

"Just get on up there before he makes everyone in the building walk on eggshells all day. Don't stand there gawking at me, girl," the receptionist said.

I stepped into the crowded elevator and pushed the right button. Third floor and he was in the first door on the right. When the elevator stopped at the first floor, a flurry of folks departed but there were none to get inside. I just stood there, frozen, until the doors closed, and the elevator began to squeak its way to the third floor.

When it stopped that time, I forced myself to get off. Then there was his door right there in front of me. It had a fancy brass plate engraved with his name. I stared at it so long that it became a blur and I had to blink. Finally, I put my hand on the knob, opened the door a crack, and peeked inside. The office was empty. Was that a sign that I should forget this whole thing and go home?

Before I could turn around and leave, a door on the other side of the room flew open and a tall man with blond hair streaked with gray hurried toward the biggest desk I'd ever seen. "What are you waiting for? Come on in here." He raised his voice. "You should have been here five minutes ago. Grab that laptop and let's get going. You're not the same girl they usually send. She sick or something?"

"I'm not sure what you mean, sir," I answered.

"Just get the laptop. We've got to be there on time." He carried a heavy briefcase. "Hurry up. What's your name, anyway?"

"Jessica."

Stunned, I picked up the laptop computer. I was already carrying my bright-red tote bag, and it contained copies of all the letters I'd found in my mother's memory box.

"We're closing on a big corporate loan today," he said as he rushed down the hallway. "I'll need you to set up my laptop for me, get coffee or whatever else the clients want, and do whatever I say. Is that understood?"

"Yes, sir." I nodded.

"My regular legal secretary had an emergency appendectomy last night. She's out of commission for a couple of weeks. You've done this kind of thing before, haven't you?" He opened the door into the conference room and stood to one side. At least he was a gentleman.

"Couple of times, sir." I'd grown up in real estate, so I understood loans.

When we reached a conference room on the same floor, he motioned for me to put the laptop in front of the chair at the head of the table. When I finished that, I checked out the beverage bar where someone had already set up doughnuts and finger foods. There was a crystal pitcher on a tray marked *Sweet tea*, an identical one marked *Unsweetened tea* and a pot full of coffee. On a separate tray there were stacks of white plates and matching cups.

My chest was tight with anxiety. His hair, plus his height and face shape, left no doubt what DNA pool I'd taken a bath in before I was even born. All he had to do was look at me and then look at himself in the mirror to know that I was his child.

A group of six men and two women filed into the room, stopped by the refreshment table to load up saucers, and then proceeded on to the table. I played glorified waitress, going from one to the next, taking their orders for something to drink. I was glad that at least I hadn't worn jeans and that I'd put on a pair of shoes instead of flip-flops.

Edward pulled a sheaf of papers from his brief-case and tightened his mouth into a firm line. I'd done that same thing many times when James was bossing me around, so evidently some things were inherited by DNA and not by environment. My poor mama—every time she looked at me, she would have remembered him.

It was close to noon before they'd covered every single fine point in the contract. The buying firm's lawyers asked all kinds of things before they finally declared everything ready to sign. The figures were more than I'd ever dealt with, but the process was pretty much the same—make sure everything is up to code and passes inspections and then sign right here to close the deal. Not that I had anything to do with any of the actual business that morning. I was just there to fetch coffee and smile.

"You were pretty good in there," Edward said when we were back in his office.

"I've worked in real estate," I said. "It wasn't my first rodeo."

"Well, I hope the agency sends you every day," he smiled. "You can take a long lunch. I've got a date with my wife and daughter, so I'll be out an extra half hour. I'll meet you in the office at one thirty."

I meant to tell him there had been a mix-up and I wouldn't be back, but I said, "I'll see you then."

When he'd said he was having lunch with his daughter, my pulse jacked up and my heart threw in an extra beat. I'd been so intent on seeing him that I hadn't thought of the child he'd had with the other woman. I had another sister—well, half sister, but still blood kin.

I had lunch right around the block from the building, just a bag of chips and a diet root beer because I was far too nervous to eat much of anything. That alone was crazy, because I'd been known to eat three chili dogs for lunch and then finish it off with a double chocolate sundae when I was antsy. Sitting alone at a table outside the tiny bistro, I kept a close watch on the clock on the outside of the bank across the street. In my normal world there was never enough time to get things done, but that morning, it took forever for the second hand to move forward a minute.

That old saying about a watched pot never boiling came to mind, so I stood up and walked around the area until I found a small park between the law firm and the bank next to it. As I sat on a bench and listened to the sounds of the ocean in the background, memories flashed through my mind of the other time we'd been in Florida—Mama, Ashley, and me. Had Mama chosen a beach an hour away because she didn't want to take even a remote chance of running into Edward?

The jogger from the night before walked past me, and I was jerked back into the present with no answers. Today he was dressed in dress slacks, a pale-blue shirt, and a red-and-blue paisley tie. He didn't even glance my way or notice that I'd tucked my feet under the bench to keep from tripping him again.

It was after one when I went back to the office, and I still wasn't sure if I should come clean or keep showing up for work every day. On one hand, I really wanted to stick around. On the other, Mama's voice in my head kept telling me to be honest.

"Hey," the receptionist at the front desk called out when I started for the elevator. "The agency got mixed up and sent another girl over this morning. Guess they forgot they told you to do the job. I sent her back. Sometimes they get so busy they don't know who they send where. You staying for a few days, or do I need to call them?"

"I don't know," I answered.

"Well, make up your mind," the receptionist

nodded. "Good morning, Mr. Rycroft." She looked beyond my left shoulder.

"Hello, Juanita. You look lovely today." He flashed a brilliant smile her way.

His deep drawl sounded familiar, but I didn't want to whip around and stare. The elevator doors opened, and I stepped inside with him right behind me.

"Two or three?" he asked.

"Three." I answered and then realized that Mr. Sexy Voice was the man who'd ruined his MP3 player on the beach the night before. His broad shoulders slimmed to a narrow waist, and he was taller than me—six feet, four inches at the least—because I had to look up at him.

"New here?" he asked.

"Just temp help." I rolled my eyes up at the fancy tiles on the elevator ceiling to keep from looking at him.

His dark brows drew down into a frown. "You look familiar."

I shrugged. "I get that often. You work in this building?"

"Yes, I do. Are you sure we haven't met?" His dark brows drew down as he stared at me.

I caught his frown in the mirrored walls just as the

elevator doors opened. If that was his best pickup line, he'd better get out the *Flirting for Dummies* book.

"I heard that Edward had to call the temp agency. Whoa! You are the woman on the beach who tripped me."

Bravo! You don't need the dummy book after all.

"That's right." I stepped out of the elevator and opened the door into Edward's suite. I needed to decide what I was going to do, and I only had maybe half a minute to do that. I didn't have time to argue with Mr. Rycroft. I had a half sister who I'd love to meet, but that might not happen if I was honest with Edward and didn't stick around.

"So, where are you from?" Rycroft followed me into the office and hiked a hip on the desk. "You have a different accent than we do around here."

"I'm from Jefferson, Texas," I answered honestly.

"Long way from home." He toyed with a pencil on the desk. "How'd you get to Florida and working for the temp agency?"

"I don't work for the temp agency." I said honestly. "I came in here to talk to Edward Rollin this morning, and he just assumed I was from that place. He demanded I pick up the laptop and follow him, so I did."

His blue eyes assessed me like I was something he'd buy at a flea market. "Why would you do that? Why didn't you just tell him that he made a mistake?"

"I thought I could talk to him on the way to the conference, but it didn't work out that way. I'm here to talk to him now." I made up my mind in that split second to do the right thing.

"Are you from the IRS?" he asked. "Or did he forget to tip you down at the greasy spoon where he likes to eat? Is that why you played a joke on him and pretended to be from the agency?"

He was even nosier than I was, and that was saying a lot. Evidently, the only way to get rid of him was to tell him the honest-to-God truth. "I came down here to meet my father for the first time."

"Honey." He spit out the endearment like a dirty word. "Edward closes more deals in the corporate field than any other man in the Florida Panhandle, but he's not a lawyer or a private investigator. You need one of those to find a lost father, not a lawyer like Edward."

"Well, sweet…heart." I deliberately dragged out the words in true East Texas brogue. "He'll sure be interested in this one—believe me."

"You better just pick up your things and get on

out of here." He opened the door and held it. "I'm going to tell Juanita not to let you past the front desk again."

I pulled the chair out from behind the desk and sat down. "I'm sitting right here until Edward returns, and that's a fact, Mr. Rycroft."

"Lady, you better gather up your stuff and get out of here before I call the police." He folded his arms over his chest and shot daggers at me.

"Go ahead. Call them, and I'll just tell them I was sitting here waiting for my father to return when you went ballistic and ordered me out," I said in my best saccharine-sweet tone.

"You're not Edward's daughter." He glared at me, his eyes starting at my hair and traveling down as far as he could go with me sitting behind the desk.

I raised an eyebrow in defiance. "Whether you believe me or not, you have to admit the story would make for some really interesting headlines if you call the cops. Edward Rollin's long-lost illegitimate daughter is carried out of his office screaming and yelling, causing a public scandal."

"So, what proof you got?" He growled.

"Enough, but it's not any of your business, Mr. Rycroft." I pinched my nose, trying to get rid of the raging headache that he'd caused with all his questions.

"Prove it," he demanded.

I pushed back the chair, rounded the end of the desk, and didn't stop until my nose was just inches from his. "I don't have to prove jack squat to you. Go away. I want to talk to Edward in private."

"I'm not going anywhere. You're some kind of con artist, and I won't leave you in an office full of important documents and files." He didn't back down. "And you better have some good, hard facts or Edward won't bat an eye at sending your cute little ass to jail."

He could stand there, squared off with me if he wanted to do so, but I wasn't getting out the letters for anyone but Edward Rollin. Suddenly, I wished I'd listened to Ashley and stayed home. Who would have ever thought I'd run into a brick wall like this, just trying to talk to the man who'd fathered me?

Rycroft came back to the front of the desk and pointed at the door. "It's your last chance."

I went back to the desk and sat down, took a fingernail file from my purse, and began to work on my nails. It was a calming gesture and it always worked. Ashley and I both learned it from our mother. When any one of us got out a fingernail file, it meant that all discussions were finished and that they wouldn't be open again until the file was put away.

"I mean it, Miss…miss…miss…" he started.

"Miss Jessica Susanne Graham," I said softly, but even I could hear the ice in my voice. "My friends call me Jessie. You may call me Miss Graham."

"Edward is my dear friend. I won't have you destroy his life with your false accusations," he said.

"I don't give a damn what you will or will not have. So why don't you go take care of what is your business and leave me alone?" I could hear every heartbeat making a whooshing noise in my ears. Could a woman my age die of high blood pressure?

"I told you, I'm not leaving," Mr. Smart-Ass Rycroft folded his arms over his chest. "This is an important business that we run here."

"And what do you think I am? A homeless beach bum?" I accentuated every word with a jab of my fingernail file right at his nose.

He leaned backward to get away from the pointed end and was about to say something else when Edward opened the door.

"What's goin' on in here?" he asked.

Neither of us answered so he raised his voice.

"Rocky, why are you arguing with the temp help?"

"This crazy fool isn't from the agency, and she's got a lot of nasty accusations." Rocky Rycroft—now wasn't that just a sexy, cute name—nodded toward me with a look meant to fry me into nothing but a greasy spot on the carpet.

"She is just a secretary from the agency." Edward chuckled. "Jessica, this is my junior partner, Rockwell Rycroft. We call him Rocky, and I think maybe you've both gotten off on the wrong foot."

"I would like to talk to you in private." I picked up my tote bag and set it on the desk. "Please," I added as an afterthought.

"Rocky can stay," Edward said.

"Have it your way," I told him.

Edward sat down in one of the two burgundy leather chairs facing the desk that would have been mine if I'd really been from the temp agency.

"She says she's..." Rocky started to blurt it out.

"You be quiet." I shook my file at him again. I must've looked pretty mean because he clamped his mouth shut like he was afraid I'd cast a spell on him and turn him into a slimy, green tree frog.

Then I asked Edward, "Do you remember Linda Graham from Jefferson, Texas?"

"Yes, I do," he nodded. "She handled a real estate deal for me a long, long time ago."

"She was my mother and she handled more than that, Mr. Rollin, and we both know it." I sure didn't want to have this discussion in front of Rocky Rycroft, but there didn't seem to be any way around it or any way to put it gently, so I spit it out. "I'm her daughter."

Edward smiled brightly. "I thought I remembered your name as Ashley. Who would have ever thought you would be tall and blond? You were just a little, bitty dark-haired girl when I knew Linda. I figured you'd turn out to be a petite brunette. Whatever are you doing down in this part of the country. And how is your mother?"

"Ashley did turn out to be a petite brunette. But I'm not her. I'm Jessica, Linda's younger daughter." I waited for the realization to hit, but it didn't.

"Oh, so Linda remarried. Well, what can I do for you, Jessica?" Edward said. "And why are you here in Florida?"

"No, Mother never remarried." Were all men this stupid? He didn't even feel an emotional pull when his own flesh and blood was standing in front of him?

"Mr. Rollin." The pent-up air that I didn't even realize I was holding in my lungs came out all at once in a long sigh. "My mother died in a car wreck a few weeks ago. When Ashley and I were going through her things a couple of days ago, we found a shoebox in her closet full of letters tied up with a faded red ribbon—from you. I have copies of the letters she wrote that you returned, as well as the ones you wrote to her, including one she never mailed."

"Is this blackmail?" he asked bluntly and leaned his head back to pinch the bridge of his nose. "Because if it is, young lady, I'll have no part of it."

Was I going to have to spell it out for him? I overcame the nagging desire to pinch the bridge of my own nose. "Blackmail has never entered my mind. I just came down here to see you. To actually look at you."

"Why?" he asked.

"Because you are my father."

Edward's eyes squinted down to small slits as he looked at me. "Just who told you that?"

"Mama did, even though she was already buried.

Read this last letter that she wrote you, the one she never mailed." I dug around in my tote bag and brought out the stack of letters. I handed him the right one. "Evidently, she had that one written and was ready to mail it when your box arrived with all the letters and cards she'd mailed to you through those three or four months you were seeing each other. It had a stamp on it, and it was sealed. I opened it."

When he finished reading it, he folded it and handed it back to me. "I had no idea. What is it that you want or expect of me?"

I put the letter with back with the others and slipped the whole stack back into my bag. "You "haven't got a thing I want or need. I got what I came after. To see the man who fathered me. Ashley begged me not to come down here. I probably should have listened to her, but I had to satisfy the curiosity. Goodbye, Mr. Rollin. I won't bother you again." I picked up my things and left without looking back.

Chapter 3

STRESS BRINGS ON HUNGER AND THE BAG OF chips I'd had an hour before had failed me, so I stopped by a sandwich shop and opted for a loaded foot-long sub, two bags of chips, and half a dozen macadamia-nut cookies. Every emotion in the universe raced through me—sadness, anger, depression, just to name the first on the list.

I wanted to throw myself down on the floor and pitch a two-year-old tantrum when I got back to my room, but the tears wouldn't come. So, I stripped out of my cute little sundress and put on my bathing suit. Tossing the room key into the paper bag with my food, I grabbed a beach towel on the way out the door. The sand was hot as I made my way through sunbathers to the less populated far end of the beach.

I flopped down, opened my beach bag, and took out the foot-long submarine sandwich, a liter of root beer, and a bag of chips. I was determined not to even think about the firm of Rollin, Smith, and Rycroft. Two bites later, the tears started flowing down my cheeks, and I couldn't swallow past the lump in my throat. Finally, I gave up and rolled the sandwich back up in the paper, stuffed it into the bag, and stretched out on my back. The only time I'd ever been too upset to eat was earlier that day, but I was determined to get over the total numbness.

"What do I do now, Mama?" I asked.

You've had your way and met your father. The ball is in his court now, but don't expect miracles, my child. I was glad that she still talked to me even though I knew it was just her voice in my head saying what I knew she would tell me if she was right there beside me.

I just needed a plan. It could be altered, if necessary, but having one would help me get through this terrible day. "I will lie out on the beach every day and choose a different restaurant every night for supper," I said out loud. "Tonight, it will be Jimmy Buffet's Margaritaville."

But the planning didn't stop the fresh tears. If I found another bottle, I would change my three wishes. My first new one would still be that Mama wouldn't have gone out to show that house that day but the other two would be different. I would wish I'd never found those letters, and that I'd listened to Mama all those years when she told me that I was better off not knowing about my father.

More tears spilled out over my cheeks when I thought about the last letter Edward had written to her. There she was pregnant with me and reading that his girlfriend of many years was pregnant, too, and knowing they would already be married when her letter arrived. He'd even mentioned that he was taking the coward's way out since he couldn't bear to hear the disappointment in her voice if he called or came to Jefferson to tell her in person, or even if he called her on the telephone. But she'd taken the high road and tucked the letter she'd written to him in with the stash that he'd returned.

"You're going to burn," a soft voice said.

I wiped my cheeks and sat up and looked into the worried eyes of a very pregnant young woman. "I wasn't asleep."

"You're Jessica, aren't you?" She was far enough along that she looked like she might have the baby right there on the sandbar in the next five minutes.

"Yes, I am. How'd you know that?"

"I'm Tamara," the woman said. "Tamara Rollin Rycroft."

"Oh, you're married to—Rocky?" So, he was married and expecting a child.

"No, ma'am, I'm married to Stephen, Rocky's brother." She sat down beside me. "Daddy said Rocky was there when you told him you were his daughter."

"What are you doing here?" This woman was my half sister. I looked at her even closer. We shared a father and DNA but not a single emotional surge of kinship chased through me. I didn't want to hug her, but then I didn't want to slap her, either.

"I'm not sure." She shrugged. "Daddy came home ago a while ago and called a family conference. Me, mother, Stephen, and him. Quite an upsetting and emotional experience for him. Mother knew that he'd been seeing another woman during the time they were dating. I guess they'd had an argument and were kind of split up when he and your mother were together. But Daddy promised Mother that it was over before they got married. Neither of them expected a daughter from that little fling to come walking into our lives after all these years later." She laid a hand on her bulging baby bump.

Fling! Maybe I did want to slap her after all. My

mother had loved Edward. What they'd had was not a fling! My breath came out in short gasps, and I gritted my teeth.

"I didn't come here to make a problem for anyone," I said. "I never gave monetary things a thought or blackmail either for that matter. I just wanted to see my father. When I was a little girl, I used to think that someday I would come home from school and there would be a car in the driveway, and it would be my father." I sat up and picked up a handful of warm sand, let it sift through my hands, and then went on. "He would have a grand story about why he wasn't there when I was a baby, and Momma would be smiling, and we'd all live happily ever after.

"Then I got into high school and convinced myself he'd died a hero's death doing some fantastic deed. Ashley—that's my older sister—her father died when he was in the army. So, in my dreams, my father died while trying to save an orphanage full of children from burning or something heroic like that. Then Mama died and I found the letters. All I wanted to do was see him. And I wouldn't have ever gone to your mother and made a scene. It's not what I came down here for."

This woman sitting next to me was a stranger.

She was tall but not as much of a giant as me. We shared the same face shape, the same brown eyes and long legs, but I felt more of a kinship to Ashley, who looked nothing like me.

"I think I understand," Tamara said after an awkward silence. "I called your sister. Daddy told us your mother owned the Graham Real Estate Agency. So, I just called there and told her who I was and what had happened today. I asked her if she knew where you were staying, and I came down here to scream and yell at you. I was going to tell you to go straight to hell and never come around and upset my family again."

"Why didn't you?" My voice was flat and emotionless, but then I felt drained.

"I sat down beside you. Figured it was you, because Daddy said you were a tall blonde and you're the only woman with blond hair right now on this stretch of beach. I tried to think about how your mother must have felt. I'm pregnant. How would I feel if Stephen didn't even know? If I'd loved him with my whole heart and he wrote me a letter saying it was over, and then there was a baby. God, I don't know what changed my mind. I guess I'm sentimental because of this baby."

"Natural red hair, huh?" I asked.

"Yep, just like my mother's," Tamara said. "Baby hasn't got a chance. Stephen is a redhead, too. You do realize that we're sisters?"

"Yes, I do, and yet we are complete strangers." I got up and made my way back to the portion of the deck that was mine.

Tamara waddled along behind me. "Daddy tells me that you met Rocky?"

"Three times." I wanted the woman to go away, not carry on a conversation with her.

She cocked her head to one side—just like I did when I was puzzled.

"He fell over my legs last night when he was jogging on the beach. I saw him at the park at noon today, but he didn't recognize me. Then this afternoon at your father's office. If I never see him again, it will be too soon. I'm going inside now. Do you need anything else?" I had a hand on the door into my room.

"I don't know," she said. "My curiosity isn't satisfied just yet. When is your birthday?"

"November one, and I was twenty-eight on my last birthday," I answered, wondering why she'd want to know that bit of information.

"Mine is December fifteenth of the same year, and I'll be twenty-eight." Tamara said. "Kind of blows my mind to know I've practically had a twin all these years."

"Anything else?" I opened the door. "We're too old and this situation is too complicated for us to be sisters, Tamara. Goodbye and good luck with the baby. I have two nephews and I love them dearly."

Tamara smiled. "Well, this is a girl, so I guess you'll have a niece now. But you're right. With the situation like it is, she'll never know an aunt Jessica."

"Don't worry. If the world shrinks and our paths should happen to cross, I won't mention it to her. Like I said before, I didn't come down here to create problems in your family."

"Well, goodbye, Jessica," she said as she turned and disappeared around the end of the building.

My phone rang the moment I was inside. I sighed when Ashley's picture popped up on the screen. The choice was mine—either take the call or have her sending the police to knock down my door.

"Did that woman who said she was Edward's daughter call you yet? I told you to leave this alone. We knew from the letter that he had a child, but I never thought of her being your age." Ashley's voice always went all high and squeaky when she was nervous. Right then, it sounded like Minnie Mouse was on the other end of the phone. "I remember when he was dating mother. I was just a little girl, and he was very nice to me."

"And you didn't tell me?" My voice went all high and squeaky.

"I didn't know that he was your father, honest," Ashley protested. "He wasn't in the picture very long, and she didn't mention him after he was gone. When I was having pancakes with a client down at the café this morning, I remembered eating there with him and Mama. He was tall, blond-haired, and brown-eyed. So did she find you or not?"

"Yes, she did. I thought she might tell me to go to hell. Ended up having a fairly decent talk and then we said goodbye," I answered.

"Probably the best thing. You've seen him and your half sister. It's over so you can come on home. James is going to slip right through your fingers, girl." Ashley changed the subject abruptly.

"I hope he does." I didn't want to think about James or relationships with anyone right then. I just wanted to curl up on my bed and eat my way through the depression.

"Will you be back to work the day after tomorrow?"

I shook my head. "I'm staying gone the full two weeks. Don't worry about me, Ashley. I'm fine. Like a smart man said centuries ago—I came. I saw. I conquered. I came down here, saw him, and conquered all those crazy mixed-up biological emotions. I'm fine, really."

"You are not fine," Ashley argued. "I can hear *not fine* in your voice. If you are really going to stay two weeks, promise me you will lie out on the beach, and you won't see him again. We both made it just fine without a father. Mama did a fine job of serving as both parents to us."

"Yes, she did, and I promise on both counts and I love you, Sister." I hung up and went back out on the deck and saw Rocky Rycroft jogging down the beach. There was no mistaking him with that body and those long strides but today he didn't have little skinny wires running from his ears to a player tucked away in his pocket. When he saw me looking at him, he veered toward the deck.

"What are you still doing here?" His looks would have terrified a less angry woman. "Haven't you stirred up enough trouble? Go on back to that

Podunk town you're from and get out of my part of Florida."

"Do you, Mr. Rycroft, own the whole panhandle and this stretch of the gulf as well?" I asked with sarcasm dripping from every word. "No one told me that. And there isn't a sign on the outskirts of town that says I can't stay here, so get out of my world, Mr. Rycroft. Don't threaten me. If you don't like to see me around, then run somewhere else the next few days."

"I'll run anywhere that I please, and if you're planning on another visit to the office, you better think again," he said.

I leaned forward on the railing. "Don't threaten me. I told you and Mr. Rollin that I wouldn't bother any of you again. I keep my word." I turned around and went into the room.

I turned on the television and watched *Steel Magnolias*. I cried at the end when the heroine died, but she reminded me of my mother—strong-willed and determined to do anything for her son. Not everything ended with a happily ever after like in the books. But it would have been nice if I'd gotten one—just this one time—even if it was only on a corny movie from years ago. I picked up the newest mystery book by my favorite author, but it couldn't keep my attention, so I laid it aside and watched a rerun of *Justified*.

An hour later, my growling stomach told me that I hadn't eaten much at all that day, so I took a quick shower and dressed in a light-yellow sundress and matching sandals. Tonight, I was dining at Margaritaville—alone—but Mama preached that a woman should always look nice when she went out to dinner.

"This evening is for me and you, Mama. I'm going to pretend you are at the table with me, and I'm going to think about all the fun times we'd had together," I said as I picked up my purse and walked out the door.

The crowd was young, the waiters lively, and the music loud. I requested a seat in the back corner so I could watch the people and ordered a margarita to sip on while I looked over the menu. Right in front of me was a big screen featuring Jimmy Buffett. Overhead was an airplane hanging from the ceiling, and a clown on stilts was going around from table to table, tying balloons into animal shapes for the children.

"Be right out." The waiter was a cute kid who barely came to my shoulder and looked even shorter beside the stilted clown. "Maybe some appetizers? The crab cakes are to die for."

"Yes, that would be great." I nodded.

He hurried across the room to another table, and I studied the menu until I figured out what I wanted and then laid it to the side. I glanced around at the people—and locked gazes with Rocky Rycroft.

Couldn't fate give me one little, tiny break? If I was going to run into him every time I went anywhere, I might as well go on home and schedule some time off later in the fall. Finally, he blinked and looked away, and I turned my attention to the clown on stilts.

Wishing you were eight years old again and could get a balloon shaped like a giraffe? Mama's voice was there again.

"Yep, I do," I muttered and stole a sideways glance back at Rocky's table.

A small dark-haired lady, Edward Rollin, and a tall, red-haired woman were around the table with him. The redhead had to be Tamara's mother, but who was the other woman?

I wasn't sure if the feelings I had were created by

anger, attraction, or maybe a mixture of both, but I determined that Rocky was not about to intimidate me. Whether he liked it or not, this happened to be a public place, and I was having the seafood platter with all the trimmings.

"Your drink and order of crab cakes." The waiter set both on my table.

"Thank you. I'll have the lobster dinner with a loaded baked potato and the salad with your house dressing." I handed him the menu.

He laid a paper coaster in front of me. "Gentleman over there asked that I give you this."

I don't know what game you're playing, but it's over. You lost. Get out of here before there's a problem too big for you to take care of. RR

"Do you need to return something?" the waiter asked.

I picked up a coaster from the other side of the table. "Take him a Texas iced tea with extra liquor in it and this note."

I wrote: *Have a Texas drink on me, and then go straight to hell.*

Rocky turned scarlet when the man set down

the coaster and a drink. I held up my margarita and winked, then ignored him as I turned my attention to Jimmy Buffett, singing "It's Five O'Clock Somewhere" on the big screen in the corner.

Movement in their area caught my eye and I glanced that way. Edward said something and they all laughed, then pushed back their chairs, tossed their napkins on the table, and filed out. Well, that was that. He was gone and I didn't have to deal with him again. At least that's what I thought until Rocky returned and picked up his wallet from the table where they'd been sitting.

As he left, he put a hand on the back of my chair and leaned down to whisper, "Stop stalking me."

"Don't kid yourself. You would be the last man in the universe that I would stalk." I looked up into his eyes and flashed a fake, sugary-sweet smile. "But thanks for the joke. I needed a good giggle today."

Chapter 4

TWO DAYS LATER, I WAS BACK IN JEFFERSON—SO much for fourteen days on the beach. I wanted to be home in familiar surroundings away from any café or beach where I might run into Rocky again. The moment I saw the city limits sign, I braked and pulled over to the side of the road. I thought about getting out and kissing the ground but figured someone would see me and it would be in the newspaper the next week. I didn't even go by my house but drove straight to the office and jogged from the car, across the parking lot, and inside the building.

"Well, look what the cats have drug up and the dogs wouldn't have." Ashley crossed the floor to give me a big hug.

"That's not a very nice welcome home." I hugged her back tightly. "God, I missed Texas. I may never leave the state again. What's happening in town? What did I miss?"

THE THIRD WISH 155

"James didn't get married so you're still in the running," Ashley teased.

"Oh, hush." I stepped back and air slapped her on the arm. "It's close enough to five o'clock that we can call it quittin' time. Let's go get a banana split. I really missed you, Sister, and you were right. I shouldn't have gone."

"Since you admitted it, I won't tell you 'I told you so.' Danny is grilling steaks, and Graham is bringing his girlfriend. Want to join us? Remember the preacher's daughter, Roseanna? She and Graham are getting thick as thieves. They'll both start high school in a few weeks. I still can't believe I'll have a child in the ninth grade, or that he has a girlfriend." Ashley turned off her computer and picked up her purse.

"Sounds great but I need to get unpacked. Would you ask Danny to bring Callie over to my place after supper?" I yawned. "It was a long drive and I'm worn out—please."

"Since you said 'please.'" Ashley grinned. "Callie told me last night she was going to live at my house since Trey pets her more than you do. I might let her stay if she would catch that pesky mouse that's been raiding my bread box."

"Oh, no! You can't steal my cat. She's my therapist. I tell her my deepest, darkest secrets."

"It's a good thing you didn't stay two weeks or else she would have refused to go home with you," Ashley teased.

The next morning, I was sitting behind my desk sipping my first cup of coffee when James breezed into the room with a box of doughnuts in his hands. "I heard that the prodigal returned home."

I rounded the desk and wrapped my arms around him. He barely came to my shoulder and had begun to lose his thin, brown hair this past year. "You missed me, and you know it. Are these maple long johns? You are a sweetheart!" I opened the box and stacked three on a paper napkin. "Well, don't just stand there pouting, tell me what you're doing today. Got any murder cases in Choctaw County? Any divorces, adoptions? Did you get married or laid while I was gone? We've got a lot of catching up to do even though it's only been a few days."

He sat down in a chair in front of my desk. "I'm not pouting."

"Yes, you are, and you were right. I shouldn't

have gone down there, but I did, and it can't be undone. But it's over. Enough about me. Ashley said you didn't get married. Are you pouting because I didn't stay gone long enough for you to find your soul mate? I know I get in the way of your love life, but it's only because I love you." I bit into the first pastry. Nothing in Florida had tasted as good as that did.

"You were gone less than a week, for God's sake!" James removed his glasses and cleaned them on a tissue he pulled from the box on my desk.

"You got laid. I can see it in your eyes. 'Fess up." I grinned so big that my face hurt.

He picked a blueberry doughnut from the box. "That is private and confidential between me and Colleen. Besides, you went running off and didn't even tell me you were going. You don't deserve to know anything that's been going on."

"Stop bellyachin' about that. I told you that you were right. Don't rub it in," I warned him and changed the subject. "No one makes doughnuts like our local bakery."

"Stop trying to talk about something else." He put his glasses on and tipped up his chin a notch. "Men do not bellyache or pout. You're the one who has PMS, a bad temper, and depressions, remember? I thought all women were like you, but I'm finding out that one particular woman can be warm and friendly and caring."

"Well, marry her. I'll go with you to pick out the engagement ring. Do I still get to be best woman at your wedding? You won't make me wear a tux, will you?" I licked a little maple sugar icing from my lip.

I've always loved bantering with James. He's been my best friend since kindergarten, where he was the shortest child in class and I was the tallest. We went to college together where I majored in business and real estate and he majored in prelaw. I came home to Jefferson after four years, and he went on to law school. I missed him and was ecstatic when he decided to take a job with a firm right there in our hometown. Through the years, he's listened to my tales of pushy boyfriends, and I've listened to him moan about all women being turned off by short men.

"I'm not ready to marry her but if I do propose, I'm not even going to tell you. I may not even let you be my best woman," he said testily.

I laid my hand over my heart. "You are going to

make me cry but, darlin', if I can't be your best man, then I won't let you be my man of honor."

"Oh?" He raised an eyebrow. "Are you tellin' me that you met someone down there?"

"I am not," I declared. "We were talkin' about your love life, not mine, and why would you ask such a stupid question?"

"Because there's something off about you. You're acting weird," he said.

"Am not." A vision of Rocky Rycroft running on the beach shot through my mind.

"Are too," James said. "I'm your best friend, remember. Since we were five years old. And even when you lied to your mother, you couldn't lie to me. So 'fess up, Jessie. What went on in Florida?"

"Nothing." I crossed my fingers behind my back. "I found Edward Rollin. Biologically, my name is Rollin, but it doesn't fit, does it? Jessica Rollin. Nope, I'm just plain old Jessica Graham. He's got a wife and a daughter who is giving him a grand-daughter any day now. And he sure doesn't want a reminder of a big mistake he made all those years ago coming back into his life right now."

"I'm not surprised." James propped his expen-sive shoes on the desk. He dusted the crumbs from the front of a western-cut, dark-brown suit tailored to fit his body. "It was a long time ago. He didn't even know about you. Must be a heck of a shock. Would be if I'd been in his shoes."

"I guess so." I checked for crumbs on my pale-yellow silk blouse and matching floral skirt. "He thought I was there to blackmail him."

"Probably would have been my first idea, too," James said. "I'd better get going. I'm due in court at ten o'clock. But this conversation is not over."

I picked up another doughnut. "If you don't show me yours, then you don't get to see mine. And how do you know it's not just being home that makes me so happy?"

"Because we are best friends."

I didn't even try to get in the last word because he was right.

Chapter 5

IN THE MIDDLE OF THE MORNING, FRED, A FAMILY friend, popped by the office. He wiped sweat from his forehead with a blue bandanna as he eased down into a chair. "I see you didn't stay in Florida for the whole two weeks. Talk around town said you went down there to meet your father. That right?"

"I did and I met him and now I'm home. What are you doing in town when the sun's out and you could be fishing?" I changed the subject.

"Coming to see the two prettiest women in the great state of Texas." Fred chuckled. Tall and lanky and always wearing bibbed overalls, he loved to fish almost as much as I did. "Thought I might sell the farm."

Ashley stepped out of her office into mine. "I've been trying to buy that land for ten years, you old codger. Don't come in here teasing me about selling it."

"Truth is…" He lowered his voice. "I come in

here to tell you there's a young whippersnapper staying out in the motel down south of town. Tall drink of water with dark hair and blue eyes. He's running a brand-new Ford Ranger truck with a Florida license plate. Got the numbers right here." He pulled a matchbook from the bib of his overalls and handed it to me. "Came down to the reservoir and dropped your mother's name. He thought he was bein' real slick. I drove through town and checked all the motels, since he said he didn't have any relations around here, and there was his truck at the hotel south of town."

"Who is he, and why would he ask about Mama?" Ashley asked.

"Said his name was Rocky, and he knows his stuff about lures and bait. But I thought maybe you'd better know there was a stranger in town bringing up Linda's name."

"Rocky?" Ashley frowned.

"I met him when I was in Florida. He works with Edward Rollin." I was surprised that I could utter a word, much less a sentence. My pulse raced and my chest tightened until it was hard to breathe. I'd left his little world and he had no business in mine, so what was he doing here?

"Who is Edward Rollin? That your father?" Fred asked. "And what has one got to do with the other?"

"Rocky works for Edward. I have no idea what he's doin' in town," I answered.

"Well, he seemed harmless. Does James know about him?" Fred eyed me closely.

I patted Fred on the shoulder. "James and I don't tell each other everything."

"Rocky said that he was goin' back to the river this evenin'. Right up under the bridge." Fred picked up a doughnut from the box on my desk and stood up. "Be seein' y'all."

"Thanks for the heads-up." Ashley waited until he was completely out of the office before she popped her hands on her hips and gave me the same look that Mama always did right before she threw a hissy fit. I threw up both palms and stood up.

"Who is this Rocky?" Ashley asked.

"He's kind of like a junior partner with Edward. I can't imagine why he'd come to Jefferson, but I'll find out. I'll get my fishin' pole and head down to the bayou and I'll call you tonight soon as I get home to tell you whatever I find out." That seemed to take some of the steam out of her attitude.

"Promise?" she asked in a low whisper.

I crossed my heart with my finger. "Yes, I promise."

I left thirty minutes early, drove straight home, changed into faded jeans and an old T-shirt, found my lucky hat, and headed out. It's only a five-minute drive from my house to the Big Cypress Bayou, but several scenarios played out in my head on the way. All of them were overly dramatic and filled with smart-ass remarks, so it was anticlimactic when I simply sat down beside him and threw my line out into the water.

"What are you doing here?" he asked.

"This is my home and my bayou and I'm fishin'. I might ask you the same question, Mr. Rycroft."

"The same as you." Rocky smiled. "And it's Rocky, not Mr. Rycroft. That makes me think my uncle Jasper is close by. He's Mr. Rycroft. I'm just Rocky. Got any good fishing tips?"

How dare he act like we were old friends or even acquaintances!

"If you are going for catfish, you might let it set there instead of reelin' it in. Catfish lay on the bottom. They don't get in a hurry about nothing. They lay there and watch that worm, and just when you think they're taking a nap, they grab the worm, hook, line, and sinker. Now if you're just working for striper, you might be doing it right. They like the chase, but you won't get stripers at this time of year. What are you really doin' here? Are you stalkin' me?"

"No, ma'am. I'm here because…" He hesitated.

"Might as well spit it out. Did Edward send you?"

"Kind of, but not really. Okay, here's the deal." He tossed his line out into the bayou and drew in a lungful of air. "Yesterday morning, Edward called a meeting of the partners. He invited me because I was there when… Well, you know."

My bobber took a couple of dives but didn't go under. Everything about him said that he didn't want to be there. No, that wasn't right. He held the rod and reel like he knew about fishing and liked it. What he didn't want was to be there with me.

"Go on," I said.

"Tamara had the baby that night after she talked to you. It was a girl, and they named her Hannah. She came home the next day, but she's got a case of that depression that some women get and a guilt complex all tied up with it. All she does is cry, and nothing Edward or Eva—that's his wife, if you didn't know—can do will help. Tamara says that she's been spoiled rotten all her life, and you probably didn't have anything. She's got this big picture of a little orphan girl with a dirty face and barely enough to eat. Eva said that someone had to come up here to Texas to get a real picture of how things are, and Tamara said that she would believe whatever I tell her because I'm kinfolks."

"Edward should have told her that my mama was a businesswoman and that Ashley and I both had a good life. Why didn't he?" I felt like Pandora did when she opened that box.

"He did! But she wants more proof—as in pictures and my daily reports. If Tamara wanted the Hope Diamond, Eva would start liquidating assets so she could put it in her hands. I'll spend a few days here and call Tamara every night. I'm glad that you decided to go fishin' tonight, so I can tell her that I talked to you." His voice wasn't as flat as I expected but held a hint of excitement.

The idea of someone snooping into my life and telling someone about it didn't set well with me. "What are you going to tell her?"

"That you like to fish," he answered. "Tamara will get over all this depression before long, according to her doctor. It could happen tomorrow, or it might take a week. But I'm here until she's happy."

Not one catty, hateful thing came to my mind. Deep down inside my heart, I hoped that it took several days, maybe even a couple of weeks until Tamara was happy again. I needed some time to figure out what it was about him that made me so angry and yet sent sparks flying around us every time we were together. I'd never felt that kind of thing before, and the mixture of emotions was both scary and exhilarating.

He finally broke the silence. "Have you lived here your whole life?"

I could tell him my life history right there and he'd report back to Tamara and possibly be gone the next day, but I held my tongue and simply nodded.

"Your mother? Was this her home, too?"

There didn't seem to be any harm in telling him Mama's history. "Mama was born down near Jeanerette, Louisiana, but her father moved the family here when she was a little girl."

"Your grandparents still live here then?" he asked.

"They're both gone now. Died when I was in high school. How about Edward's parents? Are they still living?" I turned the tables and asked him questions.

He shook his head. "Edward's father died a couple of years ago with a heart attack. His mother went when I was in middle school. She had a heart attack, too."

Maybe my doctor had been right when he told me that I should begin to eat a heart-healthy diet instead of living on junk food and doughnuts, if my fraternal grandparents both died with heart attacks. "Does Edward have heart problems?"

"He has high blood pressure from the job stress, but so far, so good on the heart problems. For the most part, he's conscious of his diet. Eva sees to that. She's a good woman and a good mother."

"Evenin'." Fred startled me when he appeared from the thick copse of trees behind us. "Are they bitin'?"

"Had a few nibbles but nothing yet," Rocky said. "Got any advice?"

Fred sat down beside Rocky and tossed his line out into the bayou. "Don't talk too loud. They'll hear you and hide."

"Never heard that before," Rocky said.

"Shhh, your bobber is dancing." Fred pointed.

No one said a word until the bobber settled down.

Fred shrugged. "Guess that catfish was just flirting with the worm."

Patience is the key to fishing. Mama loved the bayou and she loved to fish. Breathing in the night air, listening to the tree frogs, and letting all the cares of the world float down Big Cypress Creek usually calmed me right down. But that night it didn't. I was on edge, wanting to know more about Rocky Rycroft and why fate, destiny, or God had put him in my life. Whichever one had done the deed, they could take him on back to Florida. I didn't need or want him tearing up my life and my emotions.

Be careful what you wish for. Mama was back in my head with the words I'd heard her say dozens of times. *You might get it and then not know what to do with it.*

Chapter 6

I USUALLY GRAB BREAKFAST FROM THE DOUGH-
nut shop or a fast-food place on the way to work in
the morning. But after finding out about the heart
problems in my genetic background, I decided
that I should make a trip to the grocery store
Saturday morning to buy food that was good for
me. Maybe it was time to drag my running shoes
out of the back of the closet and get back into the
routine of jogging at least a couple of miles a day.

The apples looked good, but then so did the
bananas and the kiwis. I was trying to decide how
much fresh fruit I could eat before it went bad
when Rocky turned the corner and bumped right
into my cart.

"Well, we meet again," he said. "Are you sure you
aren't still stalking me?"

"Surer than anything in my whole life," I smarted
off. "And you can tell Tamara that I'm buying fruit,
but I will probably purchase a couple of candy bars

when I check out. Would you like the sales slip for proof?" If sarcasm was a virtue, I'd have just guaranteed myself a front seat in heaven.

"Not necessary," he said.

"Good," I pushed past him. "I figured you'd be eating out, not buying groceries."

"The motel has a small refrigerator and a microwave. It serves up a fine breakfast that I can't resist, but it's so full of carbs and fat that I have to be careful at lunch and dinner," he said. "I'm going to start jogging this evening. Want to join me and give me some tips on where to run?"

"Sure." How did that word get out of my mouth when what I meant to tell him was to dream on, that I was not interested in doing anything with him?

"Meet you at your office at five, then?" He smiled.

There were those sparks again. I was sure that I was the only one who could see or feel them since he didn't seem to be affected at all.

"I'll meet you at the bayou bridge at five thirty." No way was he coming to my office, not that day or ever.

"Deal." He pushed his cart around mine.

"What's the news on Tamara? Is she getting better?" I really wanted her to be well. After all, she was my half sister.

"I sent her pictures of your office and the town and told her all about our fishing experience. She's stopped crying so that's progress," he answered.

Strange as it was, I didn't feel like he was a stalker because he'd taken pictures. If it helped Tamara feel better, then it didn't upset me. Besides, I figured she would delete the pictures as soon as she'd looked at them.

"That's good." I started toward the checkout counter.

"What's good?" James turned the corner, and we had a three-cart pileup right there in Aisle 4.

I didn't want to deal with introductions but there wasn't any way around them. "James, this is Rocky Rycroft, one of the employees at Edward Rollin's business in Florida. Rocky, this is my best friend, James."

James stuck out his hand. "Right glad to meet you. What brings you to Jefferson?"

Rocky shook with him. "Fishing and doing a little bit of work for the bosses."

James glanced at the cart half full of groceries. "Plannin' on stayin' a while?"

"A week, maybe two," Rocky said. "Do you fish?"

"Sure I do. Jessie and I even cook on the banks of the bayou sometimes," James answered.

"Are you in the same business as Jessica?" Rocky asked.

"No, I'm a lawyer. What do you do?"

James started at Rocky's shoes and almost tip-toed to see all six feet, four inches of the man. I bit back a giggle when James straightened his back so he would look taller. I've seen him do that in court and also when he meets someone new that he wants to impress.

"I work at a mortgage company. We mainly do corporate loans and funding. I started out in prelaw, but it kicked my butt pretty fast, so I switched majors after the first year," he answered.

It was like two tomcats circling each other, trying to figure out the strengths and weaknesses of the other. I was proud of James for not letting a tall, hunky guy intimidate him. But then I was pleased that Rocky treated James with respect.

"Law school requires a lot of discipline and hours. I'm not sure I'd want to go through that again." James backed his cart up to let Rocky go on by. "My new girlfriend and I are having a cookout tonight. Jessie will be there. Come on over and join us. Jessie knows the way. You can follow her or ride with her, either one. I grill a mean steak and Colleen makes a chocolate cake that an angel would give up her place in heaven for."

"Love to and thanks for the invitation." Rocky disappeared around the corner.

"Now I know," James whispered.

"You rat! You could have asked me before you threw us together at one of your cookouts." I glared at him. "I'd planned to jog a couple of miles this evening."

"Too bad. Now you are going to eat steak and be nice to that guy. I can see that he rattles your nerves more than anyone has ever done before." He nudged my upper arm with his shoulder.

"Don't touch me." I moved away. "I'm officially mad at you."

He patted my hand. "I know you as well as you know you. And darlin', you can't stay mad at me for more than an hour so I'm not worried."

"You'd better be. Paybacks are a bitch, and I'm going to visit with Colleen this evening."

"While you do that, I'll be having beers with Rocky, and I'll tell him all your good points and your bad ones. Just remember, what goes around, comes around." He chuckled as he went on his merry way.

Right then, I would have traded him for a hungry wolf as a best friend.

Chapter 7

THAT EVENING, I OPENED THE CLOSET DOOR AND slung one hanger after another from one end of the rod to the other, trying to find something to wear. When I'd called James to get out of going, he'd laughed and said to wear white to show off my new tan. When I called Ashley to report on the fishing trip the night before, her mother instincts had risen to the top. She remembered the depression she'd had after Trey was born and felt sorry for Tamara.

"You are not trying to impress anyone, Jessie," I said to my reflection in the mirror. The last time I'd been involved with a man was three years ago, and James had listened to me bawl and squall for days after the fool dropped me for another woman. Was it fair to judge Rocky by that man? Probably not, but life was not fair. And besides, who said Rocky even felt the same vibes that I did? What I was experiencing was probably withdrawals from not dating or having a man to hold me in over a year. I'd get back into the dating pool and forget all about Rocky Rycroft's sexy eyes and body. A visual of him running on the beach materialized in my mind, and my heart started to race. Why had we thrown away all of those little pills Mama used for hot flashes when we cleaned out her house?

James had never steered me wrong, so I wore a white sundress with red sandals and matching red clunky jewelry that evening. Callie hopped off her perch in the window and was waiting expectantly when the doorbell rang.

"Right on time," I said when I opened the door.

"Hello. And hello to you, too, Callie." He bent down and rubbed the calico cat behind the ears. "You look lovely tonight."

I picked up my purse from the foyer table. "Me or the cat? And how did you know her name?"

"The cat is a beauty, but I was talking to you."

"Thank you. How did you know my cat's name?"

"It's on your Facebook page," he answered. "A person can learn a lot from social media. Which reminds me, Tamara asked if you would friend her." He stood up and glanced around. "You have a nice place here."

"I do, and you can report that to Tamara. Tell her

I'm not living in a cardboard box under the bayou bridge," I told him as I put my key fob in my purse. "You are parked behind my car, so you'll have to back out and then follow me over to James's place."

"We can ride together. I'll be glad to bring you home after the cookout is over," Rocky said.

"Sure, why not?" I shrugged.

Like a gentleman, he escorted me to his truck with his hand on the small of my back and opened the truck door for me. Vibes and more vibes danced around us. I was sure there would be a red print of his hand on my back for hours, but he acted like he didn't feel a thing.

"I also saw a picture of you and your sister together on your page. It's hard to believe that you are even related," he said as he slid under the steering wheel and started the engine.

I'd done one impulsive thing, and look where that had gotten me. I'd have to consider letting Tamara into my social-media world. That would mean seeing pictures of my new niece and not ever being able to know her.

"Are you the same man who wrote that hateful message on a coaster and had it delivered to my table?" I asked.

He backed out of the driveway. "Are you the same woman that sent a go-to-hell message back to me?"

"Guess we both got off on the wrong foot, didn't we? So now that Tamara is all better, when are you leaving?" I asked, not knowing now whether I wanted him to go or not.

"Edward gave me two weeks, and I don't even have to count it off as vacation. I kind of like it here. The fishin' is good, and I didn't know how much I needed some downtime. I slept like a baby the last couple of nights, so I'm going to take him up on the offer. Which way do I go?"

"Turn left at the stop sign. Go six blocks and turn right. It's the second house on the right, the one with the white railing around the wide porch." I pointed ahead to the stop sign.

When we arrived, James must've heard the truck door slam because he yelled over the fence, "We're all back here. Y'all come on in."

Jessica led the way through the gate and James waved her over to where he was grilling. "Hey, everyone, this is Rocky Rycroft. He's in town for a few days. Rocky, this is Jessie's sister, Ashley, and her husband, Danny. These guys here are their sons, Trey and Graham. And this is my Colleen." He slung an arm around a woman who looked up at him with adoring eyes.

I'd seen her around the courthouse when I went there to see James. I had to admit to a little bit of jealousy when he said *my Colleen*. Had things really happened that fast between them, or was this one of James's stunts to make me jealous?

Danny motioned for Rocky to join him and the other guys at the grill, and I joined Ashley and Colleen at the picnic table.

"So?" Ashley asked.

"So what?"

"What's going on with him? Wasn't he supposed to be sure you weren't living on the streets and eating out of garbage cans, then get out of Jefferson?" Ashley asked.

"Now he's decided to stay the full two weeks that they offered him. He likes the fishin'," I rolled my eyes toward the stars just beginning to pop out around a full moon.

"The way he keeps stealin' glances over here, it looks to me like he's interested in more than fishin'." Colleen smiled. "Not that I blame him. White looks really good on you. I'd love to be able to tan like that. I just burn and freckle. And to have your height… Oh, my goodness, I'd give a lot for that."

Ashley patted her shoulder possessively. "If you were any taller, you wouldn't look so cute with James."

The aroma of grilled food drifting across the yard made my stomach set up a growl. "Sorry, I haven't eaten much today."

"Hey, James," Ashley called. "She's gettin' hungry. Either hurry up or put on another steak."

"Or send Rocky out to kill an extra bull," James said, laughing.

"That is *enough*." I said without a hint of a smile.

"Be warned, Rocky." James ignored me and went on. "She can put away enough to feed Sherman's march to the sea when she's just snacking. When she's really hungry, it's Katy bar the door."

Colleen shook her head. "If I was you, I don't know if I'd poison him on Monday and watch him die a slow and torturous death or kill him graveyard dead instantly. But please don't do either one because my good black suit is too tight, and I don't want to attend his funeral. Besides, I really like him, and it would be nice to keep him around a while longer."

"Sometimes his Harley-Davidson mouth gets ahead of his tricycle butt, but I can see he's met his match." I smiled across the table at her. The way she looked at him assured me that this was not a joke James and Ashley were playing on me, but very easily could be love at first sight. Just because I didn't believe in such fantasies didn't mean they couldn't happen for other people.

James and Danny pushed a second picnic table up to the end of the one where we were sitting, making plenty of room for the eight of us. Four on one side; four on the other. Even with a foot of space between us, I could feel the chemistry when Rocky sat down beside me. The temperature jacked up a few degrees every time his leg brushed against mine under the table. When his fingers grazed mine as he passed the bread basket or the salt and pepper, I got a jolt all the way to my toes. I wanted to shake my fist at the sky and tell God that this was not fair—that He should send someone else into my life.

Rocky would go home soon and forget all about me, so I wanted the evening to be over. But at the same time, I loved the chemistry between us, and I wanted it to last forever.

At the end of the evening, I didn't expect him to walk me to the door but he did. Before I could get the key out of my purse, he caged me in with a hand on each side of my shoulders. I barely had time to moisten my lips before his eyes fluttered shut and his dark lashes lay on his high cheekbones like a fan. Then his mouth was on mine and the whole world stood still. We were the only two people in the state of Texas. Everyone else vanished—right along with my determination to never trust another man. When the kiss ended, he stepped back and traced my lips with his finger.

"Thank you for a lovely evening. I like your friends and your family," he said. "They are all good people. You are lucky to have them in your life."

"Want to come inside for a cup of coffee?" I hoped that he couldn't hear the breathlessness in my voice.

"Love to." He nodded.

He followed me into the kitchen and filled the coffeepot while I measured out the grounds. My living room, kitchen, and dining room are all one open area, so while we waited for the coffee to perk, he laced his fingers into mine and led me to the sofa where he pulled me down beside him.

With my hand in his, I swear the temperature in the room jacked up another ten degrees—maybe fifteen. "I've been askin' questions, meeting your family and friends and finding out things about you. It's your turn."

My mind was flipping around like little kids on a jungle gym. My turn to do what? Lead him to the bedroom? Kiss him some more?

Ask questions about him or Edward, that niggling voice in my head shouted.

"Okay." I said slowly, trying to get my thoughts together. "Does Tamara work in the mortgage agency?"

"No, she has a degree in elementary education. She loves kids and teaching, but she's taken time off to be a stay-at-home mother until Hannah is at least a year old. It could stretch until Hannah goes to preschool, though. I don't expect her to go back to work anytime soon because she wants at least four kids. She says that having an only child is the worse decision parents can make."

"I know what she means. I felt like an only child when Ashley went off to college. So does Edward's wife work in the agency?"

"Nope, Eva's a CPA, but she only worked until Tamara was born. Ever since Tamara and I were little kids, she's stayed home. She does charities and clubs and jumps when Tamara whines. But

Tamara's got a pretty decent nature even with all the spoiling. Eva dotes on her. And the new baby, Hannah, is going to be so rotten the garbageman won't even carry her away." He laughed.

"Whew." I whistled through my teeth. "The lifestyles of the rich and famous. What about you? Are you so rich that they jump when you holler 'froggy'?"

"My folks are what you'd call comfortable, I guess. Mother is a nurse. Daddy is an engineer. Uncle Jasper was my idol, so that's why I went into the business. My sister is doing her internship at the hospital right now. She's going to be an emergency room doctor. She's about Ashley's size, which is kind of small to be taking on the druggies and Saturday-night gang fights, but she's pretty spunky," he answered.

"Really, she's short when you are what? Six four?" My eyes traveled from his toes to the top of his head.

"She's a small person like Mother. I'm tall like dad. Six five to be exact. You saw my sister that night at Margaritaville. She was the dark-haired lady who sat beside me."

So, it wasn't a girlfriend but his sister. It wasn't the first time I'd been wrong, but I did feel pretty danged foolish.

"Tell me more about Edward," I said.

"What about him? He's close to sixty now. He was about thirty when he and Eva married, and Tamara was born a few months later. They'd dated off and on for years. She had a temper, and she was very jealous. Still does and still is, but he loves her. They're a good family, Jessica, and he's a good man."

The coffeepot stopped gurgling. I started to pull my hand free, but he held on, stood up with me, and together we went back to the kitchen. I poured with my free hand, and then he led me back to the living room and we sat down on the sofa again.

"Now let's talk about us," he said. "I understand why you went into real estate, but did you ever want to do anything else?"

"I wanted to be a horse trainer when I was eight. Does that count?"

He leaned over and kissed me on the cheek. "A woman after my own heart. I wanted to join the circus and ride bareback on horses when I was about that age."

We talked about crazy things, important stuff, ambitions, hopes, and goals until after midnight. He kissed me good night, and I closed the door, then slid down the backside. I wrapped my arms around my knees and wished that I'd met him in different circumstances.

But maybe he was what I needed right then. He was the perfect candidate for a two-week fling. No muss, no fuss. Just a wild adventure to get him out of my mind and then he'd be gone, leaving me with nothing but some hot, steamy memories. It would be one of those consenting-adult affairs, but I wasn't that kind of woman. Never had been and I couldn't start now. Either a relationship meant something, or I didn't fall into bed with a guy.

———

Callie was curled up next to me the next morning when I awoke and the sun coming through the window warmed my face. I could feel someone staring at me, and for a moment, I didn't know if Rocky was propped up on an elbow right beside me or if I'd only been dreaming. Slowly, I slid an eye open.

Ashley was sitting in a chair beside the bed. My eyes popped open so fast that a pain shot through my head. "What are you doin'? Tryin' to give me a heart attack?"

"You've got a strong heart." Ashley laughed. "At

least you used to. It might be weakened by now. I heard that Rocky didn't leave until after midnight. I'd like details."

"Go away." I rubbed my eyes. "I'm not talking to anyone until I've had two cups of coffee, a bagel, and maybe a piece of the cake I brought home last night."

"Always been an old bear early in the morning. Must have got that from Edward Rollin since me and Mama woke up happy every day." She picked up Callie and the cat went limp in her arms.

"Just go away and let me sleep until noon."

"You are going to get up and go to church with me and my family. Danny asked Rocky to join us and to come to Sunday dinner at our house. We're having pot roast and hot yeast rolls, and I even made two pecan pies."

I pulled the covers over my head. Skipping church was not an option—not unless we were sick nigh unto death. Mama made sure of that even after we were grown, and now that she was gone, Ashley had taken on the responsibility.

I moaned, "Send me back to Florida where nobody knows me."

Ashley yanked the quilt off me. "Get up and get dressed. We've got one hour until services start.

You can tell me what happened last night while you dress. Coffee is already brewing. I'll bring you a cup while you get your eyes open, and if you have time, you can have a bagel."

I sat up and yawned. "You probably already know everything that happened, so why did you wake me up? I can't sneeze in this town without a dozen folks calling you to see if I'm sick."

Ashley sat down beside me. "I want to know if he makes your heart do double time or if he gave you a case of the vapors. You know, like James doesn't do. I want to know if you're going to fall in love with Rocky, and I want to know if I need to invest in tissue stock. Because if he breaks your little heart, then you'll use up enough tissues blowing your nose that I could make a few dollars. Remember what happened when the last feller broke up with you for the tattoo queen?"

"Don't remind me." I stood up and raked my hands through my tangled hair. "I hated Rocky at first. You know that. I told you what an egotistical, pompous ass he was. But maybe we got off on the wrong foot. He's really a nice guy, but I'm not going to fall in love. I've only known him a week, and most of that we spent not even liking each other."

I did not want to go to church. I sure didn't want to be crammed up in a pew with Rocky next to me if he showed up. I needed a few hours to digest everything that had happened, to think more about Tamara and Edward, and to analyze all the things that Rocky had told me.

Chapter 8

ROCKY DID SHOW UP AT CHURCH, AND HE SAT SO close to me that every time I took a breath, I got a whiff of his expensive cologne. He came to Sunday dinner and then drove me home. It didn't seem awkward when he held my hand from his truck to my porch where he eased down on the swing and pulled me down beside him. "Dinner was amazing. I could get used to this lifestyle. I like your brother-in-law and your sister, and their boys are great."

"Oh really? Wouldn't you miss jogging on the beach, the sound of the ocean, and wearing your fancy ties?" I asked with more sarcasm in my tone than I really meant.

He shrugged. "Maybe, but I do like fishin' in the bayou, and I don't miss five o'clock traffic."

"You'd be bored in six months if you made a change. Home is home and always will be. I like the beach and the sound and smell of the ocean, but it only took a few days before I was homesick."

He stood up and stretched. "I'm going to my hotel and taking a long nap before we go jogging this evening. Meet you at the bridge, like we were going to do last night before James invited us to the party?"

"I'll be there." I covered a yawn with the back of my hand. "Five thirty. Bring your fishing gear, and we'll see if anything is biting after we go for a run. You'd best be careful, though. They say that once you eat catfish from the bayou in Jefferson, you'll always want to come back here."

"I'll take my chances." He chuckled and waved.

Callie rubbed around my legs when I went into the house and followed me to the bedroom where we both curled up on the bed for a Sunday afternoon nap. She went right to sleep, but even though I closed my eyes and counted to a hundred four times, I couldn't fall asleep.

My phone rang and I grabbed it from the nightstand. Man, was I glad to see James's picture come up on the screen. I answered it on the second ring.

"Hey, what's going on?"

"We're havin' supper on the bayou. I'll bring the cauldron and oil. We'll fry up whatever we catch right there on the banks. You bring the potatoes and Rocky," he said. "Six thirty sounds good. Oh, and the mosquitoes are gettin' worse. Bring some of those candles that keeps them away."

"We were plannin' on going fishin', so we'll meet you in our usual spot. We're goin' for a run first." With James around, it wouldn't be so hard to trust myself not to drag Rocky back in the shadows, or maybe even go skinny-dippin' with him in the bayou.

———

A hot breeze blew across my face that evening, and I tucked a long strand of hair back into my ponytail. The black cast-iron cauldron perched on a rack was filled with hot bubbling oil, ready for the first fish to be tossed in. One of my granny's patchwork quilts was spread out on the ground with citronella candles on each corner.

"I caught the first one," James yelled a few feet down the bayou.

"Is it big enough to fry?" I asked.

"Oh, yeah. Six more like this and we'll have supper," James said.

"Ever done this before?" I asked Rocky, who was sitting only a few feet away to my left.

"Nope, done lots of fishing but I've never cooked

them right by the water," Rocky answered. "You all do it often?"

"A couple of times a year." My bobber disappeared under the water but then came back to the surface. "More often when we were teenagers. There's not a lot to do in Jefferson, other than fish and steal watermelons."

"You stole watermelons?" His tone said that he didn't believe me.

"Hey, I was the best one of the whole group of us at figuring out which ones were ripe. We'd bring them down here under the cypress and willow trees and cool them in the water while we fished. They would be cold enough to be our dessert after we ate fried fish, hush puppies, and potatoes for supper. Didn't you ever do anything illegal?"

"I didn't steal." He frowned.

"Well, pardon me." I did one of those head wiggles that annoyed both Mama and Ashley. "Know where we stole most of our melons? Right out of Fred's patch. He'd rant and rave and carry on like he was going to kill the next kid who even looked at his fields, but I overheard him telling Mama years later that he watched us lots of times and thought it was a hoot because I was right in the middle of all of it."

Another frown. "You stole from your family friend?"

"Sure. Stole the worms out of his old hog lot, too. He even helped me dig them up, sometimes. This is not the big city." I gave him another head wiggle.

"Redneck paradise," he growled.

"You got it!" I smiled.

He pulled in a nice-sized catfish and yelled, "I got a big one!"

James's voice floated back through the darkness. "Great. Just a few more and we'll clean them up and throw them in the hot grease."

"Don't knock my paradise until you've lived here and raised kids in this area," I told him as I reeled in a bass about the size of his catfish.

"I'm not knockin' it, darlin'. You just surprise me more every day. I'm wondering just how many layers there are to Jessica Graham," he said.

"More than you've got time to figure out in two weeks." The way he drawled *darlin'* made my hands sweaty, and the fish almost got away from me when I took it off the hook.

"Hey, we got enough with what y'all got." Colleen carried a stringer and a big plastic bowl of cornmeal mixture to roll the fish in once they were cleaned and cut into steaks. "Let's fry them, and if we're still hungry, we'll catch some more. You got the potatoes, Jessie?"

I pulled a bag of frozen french fries from a tote bag and handed them to James. "There's another one in there if we need them."

"Okay, here we go." James dropped the first pieces into the bubbling oil.

"How do you know when they're ready?" Rocky asked.

"They float." I got out a roll of paper towels and plates. "Then we grab them out with tongs and let them drain for a minute on a paper towel and cool enough that they don't burn us too bad. We use the cornmeal we roll the fillets in to make hush puppies."

"Jessie is not patient. She's always burning her tongue." James said. "She never could wait for anything to cool."

"Well, you aren't known for your patience, either," I countered, but my mind was really on the fact that the hottest fish in the world couldn't compare to the heat on my lips the night before when Rocky kissed me.

"No stories about me tonight, or I'll start tellin'

what I know about you." I threatened him and then wondered if Mama and Edward ever came down here to fish. Was he the only man other than Ashley's father to make her heart flutter in that crazy way? Or had there been other men in her life?

"What's goin' on with you, Jessie. You went quiet suddenly." James reached for the tongs and pulled the first floating chunks of fish from the pot.

"Just thinkin' about Mama. But let's test that fish and see if you've lost your touch." I managed a smile, but my heart hurt for my mother and what she'd sacrificed all those years when she had to be both mother and father to me and Ashley.

Chapter 9

I WAS RUNNING ABOUT TWO MINUTES LATE ON Monday morning. Carrying breakfast in one hand and a file I'd taken home with me over the weekend in the other, I backed into the office expecting Ashley to be standing there pointing at the clock. But Rocky came out of her office instead.

"Good morning." He hurried to take the file from my hands and lay it on my desk. Instead of his usual jeans and T-shirt, he wore dress slacks, a pale-blue shirt, and a tie.

"What are you doing here?"

"I'm your help until Friday." He smiled brightly.

"Who said?" Where was my sister and how did he get into the office? Did he have a key?

"Ashley called me last night. Danny was able to get a week off on short notice, so they decided to take a road trip with the boys. She said to tell you that what goes around comes around and that she'd call you from the hotel tonight. They're going to

Great Wolf Lodge Resort over near Dallas. She says they'll be home sometime Friday, but she won't come back to work until Monday. She hired me to show up here every day and help you out with whatever you need," he said.

"I can't believe this." To see him in the evenings was one thing. To spend all day with him was another. Not falling for him was getting harder and harder by the hour as it was.

"I'm not a Realtor but I do know a lot about the business since I am in financing, and to tell the truth, I was getting bored with nothing to do every day until you got off work," he said.

My sister had not had a vacation since they'd taken the boys to Disney World back when they were still little guys. And I did deserve this kind of treatment after I'd left her alone for almost a whole week. But that did not mean she wasn't going to get a piece of my mind when she called that evening.

"Okay, then." I sighed. "We've got four houses to show this morning. Two down in Marshall, one here in Jefferson, and a farm up around Kildare. What's your choice to start with?"

"I'll take the farm," he said.

"You sure about that? What do you know about farms?" I tilted my head to one side.

"Tamara does that, and so does Edward." He chuckled.

"Does what? Ask you about farms?"

"No, they tilt their head to one side like you just did when they question someone," he answered. "And for your information, I probably know more than about houses since we buy a lot of that kind of land up north of Panama City for corporations to build business offices and apartment complexes," he said. "I'll take the prospective buyers for a look, buy them lunch on the way home, and wine and dine them a little."

"It sounds like you'd be pretty good at this business."

He tipped an imaginary hat. "Thank you, ma'am. Now give me a little background on the interested buyers so I know where they'd like to eat and what to talk about with them."

The phone rang before I could answer him. I picked it up and said, "Graham Real Estate."

"Are you spittin' tacks?" Ashley asked.

"Yes, and we will talk about this later." No way was I discussing Rocky with her, not with him standing right there.

"You deserve this after the way you left me alone when you went off on your Florida lark," Ashley said.

"I agree with you, Sister, but I'm busy right now. And you are in big trouble for this, so don't think that I'm going to forgive you easily."

"Either admit that you do more than like him, or kick him back to Florida."

"What did you just say?" I asked.

"Trust me, darlin'." She chuckled. "Have a good week. I'll call at least once a day." The phone went dark, so I laid it back on my desk.

"Ashley?" Rocky asked.

I nodded, not sure if I wanted to kick him back to Florida or not. "The Nelsons will be here in fifteen minutes. They're in their forties, and they sold a piece of property out on the West Coast. They must have gotten a fortune for it, and they want to reinvest their money in a farm. He was a banker. She was a nurse out there. Now they want to grow organic vegetables and raise chickens. Take them to Bubba's Barbecue for dinner and bring me the receipts."

"Okay." He sat down in the wingback chair on the other side of the desk, leaned forward, and propped his elbows on the edge of the desk. "I talked to my sister last night. Told her I had a heart problem."

My own heart dropped to my toes. Wasn't that just a kick in the seat of the pants? I'd let myself start to fall for a man who was going to die.

He smiled and went on. "I'm afraid I either have to get over you, or we have to work out some kind of deal. I've never felt like this about another woman. So what are we going to do?"

"I have no idea." I'd held my breath so long that my chest ached. "Does Edward know how you feel? We haven't known each other long enough…" I let the sentence hang there between us.

"Yes, he does, and funny as it may seem, he told me he understands completely."

"Really?" My voice was all high and squeaky.

"That's right. He's the one that fell in love with your mother, and she was from here," Rocky answered.

Love?

Sweet Jesus! I was thinking about more kisses and possibly a little fling. Not love, for God's sake.

I nervously straightened my desk. "He would never let you stay in the company if we had a relationship of any kind. His wife would string you up from the nearest oak tree."

"We'll have to figure out which bridges we need

to cross and which ones we need to burn this next week, I suppose. I've laid my cards on the table, and there's not even one up my sleeve." He dangled his shirtsleeve to show me. "So now it's your turn. Do you feel the chemistry between us, Jessica?"

"I'm not so sure that I can put into words how I feel about this attraction between us. I agree that we need to figure it out, but there are sure a lot of obstacles in our path. You sure you want to try to jump over them?" I looked right into the depths of his blue eyes.

"I've got real long legs." He rounded the desk and kissed me on the forehead.

Chapter 10

WE DIDN'T NOTICE THE BIG BLACK CLOUDS floating quietly in from the southeast and didn't see the moon disappear. We were sitting under the pavilion at the city park, and when the first loud clap of thunder rumbled above our heads, we jumped to our feet in a hurry and ran toward his truck. We didn't make it before a downpour of huge raindrops drenched us.

"Whew, talk about a fast storm." Rocky put the truck in reverse and backed away from the park. "Where did that come from anyway?"

"Who knows? Storms can come up fast and then leave us with nothing but more mosquitoes and high humidity in this part of the world." The rain wasn't cold, but the icy air from the truck's air conditioner made my damp skin feel like I'd been rolled in ice cubes.

"Cold?" he asked. "Would it be all right if we go to the motel first, so I can change out of these wet clothes? Or do you want me to drop you at the house, and I'll change and come back. It's too early to call it an evening. We could maybe watch a movie together."

"Motel first," I answered.

It wasn't far to the place where he was staying. When he parked in front of his room and hopped out, I followed him.

"I'm not sitting in the pickup with lightning flashing all around me," I said.

He nodded and ran through the raindrops to open the door. "I hate to be damp. Don't mind being wet but hate to be damp. I bet you are chilled." He shivered, grabbed a big white towel and wrapped it around my shoulders. Then he gathered up dry clothing and disappeared into the bathroom.

Pulling the towel tighter around my shoulders, I scanned the room. The bed was made, his clothes neatly hanging on the rack. Shaving equipment was lined up on the vanity, and he'd even taken time to unload his suitcases into the dresser drawers. Would he be that kind of lover? The same routine every time?

To get my mind off that visual of him tangled

up in sheets, I picked up the remote and turned on the television. Somehow, even the reruns of *The Golden Girls* couldn't take my mind off Rocky and wishing I was brave enough to march into the bathroom and share a shower with him.

"Your turn." He finally came out of the bathroom looking like a cover model for a romance book with water droplets on his dark hair and wearing lounging pants and a muscle shirt.

"I don't have dry clothes so…" I let the sentence hang.

"You can wear my sweatpants and one of my T-shirts," he offered.

"Rocky, I can't stay in this room much longer, or by morning there will be a whole bevy of shotgun-toting folks beating on your door. There will be a preacher amongst them carrying a marriage license, and you'd have to make an honest woman out of me," I teased.

"Still your turn." He opened a drawer and handed me a pair of gray sweats and a Gator T-shirt. "There's another towel right there."

If I called his bluff and came out of the bathroom with one of those skinny motel towels wrapped around my naked body, it would be all over but the afterglow. And when that died away, there would be plain old nothing.

"Those towels are made for short, skinny women." I laughed.

He turned rapidly and gathered me into his arms. The suddenness of his actions, the breathtaking aroma of the woodsy aftershave, and the passionate kiss made me change my mind about going home. I fell backward onto the bed and pulled him down with me. I tasted the bitterness of the lotion that he'd gotten on his lips and breathed in a mixture of soap, shampoo, and what was just naturally Rocky Rycroft. The thrill of his arms around me erased everything but the aching desire in my body to be satisfied. I didn't care what anyone in town thought of us spending the night in his motel room.

Afterward, I curled up with my head on his shoulder and my hand in the soft hair on his chest and closed my eyes. I wanted to hold on to this amazing feeling forever. I awoke at dawn and wondered where Callie was at first, then I remembered the amazing night that we'd had. Rocky's arm was still around me and now his leg was thrown over mine.

I kissed him on the cheek. "Hey, we've got to get up. It's daylight."

He opened his eyes and flashed a smile that lit up the whole room. "I vote we stay in bed all day."

"Sounds good to me, but Ashley might get real upset if we miss those four showings that we have scheduled for today." I snuggled even closer to his side.

He moved his leg and groaned. "I'm starving. Let's get dressed and have breakfast. The hotel started serving thirty minutes ago. Afterward, I'll take you home in plenty of time to get ready for work."

There's an old adage that says that one might as well be hanged for a sheep as a lamb, so I thought why not? There was no way that everyone in the small town of Jefferson wouldn't know that I'd spent the night with the feller staying in the hotel down south of town and working at Graham Realty. If they didn't know by midmorning, then Gloria Jane, the person who ran the breakfast buffet at the hotel, would be off work and her cell phone would be smoking.

"I'd love some biscuits and gravy." I smiled at him.

———————

The sun was barely up when he drove me home, walked me to the door, gave me a quick peck on the lips, and said he'd see me at the office. He whistled all the way to his truck, and when I reached the office that morning, he was sitting in one of the chairs in front of my desk. The aroma of coffee brewing filled the whole front office, and there was a box of cookies from the bakery on the table beside the pot. This wasn't such a bad setup.

"Good morning," he said. "Coffee is made, and I bought cookies for a midmorning snack and to celebrate selling at least one property today."

I dropped my tote bag on the floor behind my desk and rounded the end to lean down and kiss him. "I want to make supper for us tonight for a real celebration," I said. "After work you can go to the hotel and change into jeans and a comfortable shirt and meet me back here."

"Where are we going? A picnic at the river?"

"It's a surprise. The food will be simple but, darlin', the atmosphere will be heavenly. Trust me." I gave him another kiss, this time on the cheek.

He dragged me down into his lap. "Darlin', I don't care if we spend the night in a pup tent on the edge of the bayou and have bologna sandwiches on stale bread. As long as I can spend it with you, I'll be happy."

He kissed me again, and I tasted toothpaste mixed with cinnamon cookies. Not a totally bad combination.

"If I don't get up out of your lap, Mr. and Mrs. Spenser are going to find me in a very compromising situation," I whispered.

"Then lock the door and put a sign on it." He laughed. "Tell me again who these people are that we're seeing first thing."

"They're putting their house on the market, and Millie Spenser is never late to anything." I stood up and walked away from my desk. "They have five sons and five daughters-in-law, and they're sick of their kids fighting over who's going to inherit their property so she and Willard—that's her husband— are going to sell out and buy a motor home. They swear they're going to spend every penny they have before they die. And here they are." I nodded toward the door.

"Hello, Jessie, you think you can find a buyer for our house in the next month?" Millie asked.

"I imagine I can if you are serious," I answered.

"This time I'm not changin' my mind. God, I wish I'd had daughters like your mama instead of boys who brought home bickerin' daughters-in-law."

Millie slumped down in a chair and started telling us all about her kids.

"Wow," Rocky exclaimed when they left. "I know more about her than I do my own family."

I laughed out loud. "That's the way it is in small towns, and I'll be surprised if she doesn't haul Willard in here within two weeks and take the house off the market. This happens about once a year, and everyone knows that when it comes right down to it, Millie and Willard wouldn't sell their home for a million bucks," I explained.

"I've heard of small-town politics, but this is the first time I've been in the middle of it." Rocky grinned.

"Isn't it grand?" I winked.

He combed back his perfect dark hair with his fingertips. "How do you remember all of it? If I lived here twenty years, I'd still be trying to figure out all the ins and outs."

I nodded sympathetically. "When I was in Florida, I would pass someone on the strand, and I couldn't say, 'Good morning, Mary Ruth. How's your new granddaughter?' because I didn't know a soul down there."

I opened my laptop to add the Spensers' house

to my listings. "Millie and Granny canned pickles together. I know all five of their sons. Momma dated one of them before she fell in love with Ashley's daddy. But I don't know the people in your world. And if we're totally serious, Rocky, can either of us leave the comforts of our background to go to a place we're not suited to? If you came here permanently, would you someday resent me for it? I don't want to live anywhere but right here. It's something we'd better think about before we let our emotions get out ahead of our common sense."

"But what do we do about the fireworks when you lean across the desk and kiss me? Tell me, Jessica, how do we convince our hearts that our bodies don't want to cooperate?"

"I don't know, but we'd better figure it all out before we both get our hearts broken."

Chapter 11

I LOCKED THE OFFICE DOOR AT FIVE O'CLOCK AND Rocky drove me home. "I'll be ready when you get back."

"Where are we going?" he asked.

"This is my surprise, so you have to do what I say and not ask any questions."

"Yes, ma'am." He nodded. "My fate is in your hands."

I fed Callie, and I'd packed a few things inside a huge straw purse. I changed into a pair of faded jeans and a T-shirt, then tucked my small makeup kit from the bathroom into my purse. I locked the door and sat down on the porch to wait. Rocky's truck rumbled into my driveway a few minutes later and I jogged out to it, not giving him time to get out. He had changed into jeans, a pair of athletic shoes, and a knit shirt with three buttons at the neck.

"Turn left at the next corner and head north out of town," I told him.

We drove for five miles in comfortable silence. He was sure a trusting soul. I could have been taking him to the woods to kill him and bury him.

"Really, now. Where are we going?" he asked.

"We're almost there. Make the next right." My big two-story farmhouse was finally visible in the distance, sitting alone, like a silent sentinel set back in a grove of pecan trees.

"Who lives here?" he asked.

"I do." It had been several weeks since I'd been to the farm, as we called it, and I was suddenly overcome with the urge to rush. "This is my grandparents' place. They left it to Mama, who deeded five acres and the house it sits on to me for my twenty-first birthday because I loved it so much. The rest of the land belongs to Ashley. She and Danny run about a hundred head of Angus out here."

When he stopped, I hopped out of the truck before he could get around the truck and open the door for me. Taking his hand, I tugged it toward the house. "Come on. I can't wait to show you the inside." I found the right key and unlocked the door.

"Do you do this often?" he asked.

I stopped in the middle of the foyer. "No, Rocky, I don't. I come here when I have a long weekend and I bring Callie. We pretend we're back in the nineteenth century. But no, this is the first time I've ever brought a man to this house, if that's what you're asking me."

"Thank you." He smiled. "That makes me special."

"Yes, it does," I told him.

"You mentioned us cooking. I'm starving, so show me to the kitchen and tell me what I can do to help."

"We're having spaghetti, French bread, and Asti wine. Then we're having strawberry shortcake for dessert with real whipped cream. After that, I planned on a movie." I dropped my purse on the foyer table. "And yes, you can help me cook."

He seemed to be taking everything in when we reached the huge country kitchen, but what caught his attention most were the windows overlooking the backyard and wooded area where two white-tailed deer fed on the green grass.

He pointed and whispered, "Do you see that, Jessica?"

"They come up most evenings. Callie likes to fuss at the squirrels in the pecan trees. They are taunting her, because if she could catch one, she would have it for supper. They're lucky there's glass between them." I took a skillet from the cabinet and threw in a tablespoon of butter. When that melted, I diced onions and peppers straight into it. "You can set the table. We'll watch the wildlife while we eat."

He slipped his arms around my waist and kissed me on the neck. "Why do you live in town when this is here?"

"I always thought I'd move out here after Grandpa died, but my house in town is so close to work. Maybe someday." I loved his warm breath on my neck, but if he didn't take a step back, we weren't going to have supper at all. We'd wind up in the bedroom and forget all about everything else.

I moved away from him, took an apron down from a hook, and tied it around my waist. "Dishes are in that cabinet. When you get the table set, go look around the place. The living room is across the foyer. The den is behind that. Sun porch is wonderful this time of evening, if you want to unwind and watch the deer and the squirrels. There are four bedrooms upstairs. One for Granny and Grandpa, one for Ashley, one for Mama, and the yellow one is mine."

"You lived here?" he asked.

"Until I was about four and Momma bought her own place in town. Ashley was old enough to watch me in the summers by then, and Granny's health was beginning to fail, so I guess I was too much for her to keep up with." I added meat to the sizzling onions and peppers and put a pot of water on the back burner.

He gave me a butterfly kiss on the cheek and quickly set the table. I could hear doors opening and closing as I finished up the simple supper. It was dusky dark, the twilight of a summer evening, when we finished dessert and Rocky pushed his chair back.

"That supper was amazing, and the view both inside here and out the window is priceless." He reached across the table and covered my hand with his. "Now, does the maid come in and do the dishes, or can I help with them?"

"I never turn down help," I answered. "But we'll just put them in the dishwasher. Granny insisted on all the modern conveniences, and even Grandpa, as gruff as he could be, would never cross Granny. 'Cause if Granny wasn't happy, wasn't nobody happy."

"Well, we can't have an unhappy granny. Do you realize this would be the absolute perfect place to raise a family?"

Love.

Family.

The things I wanted most in life and was too afraid to even say the words out loud. "Of course, it would. Mama was raised here and so were Ashley and I up until we moved into town."

I carried dishes to the cabinet. He rinsed them and put them into the dishwasher. Then he circled my waist with his arm, and together we went to the living room to watch a movie. I would much rather have gone straight upstairs, but tonight it was about us being together more than just about having wild, passionate sex.

I sat down beside him on the couch, snuggling down into his shoulder with a sigh. This was the way I'd like to spend all my evenings—a nice dinner after work, maybe a movie, or when it wasn't so hot, we'd sit on the porch while the kids ran out the last bit of a day's worth of energy. It was a fairy tale, but it was my story and that evening I could tell it any way I wanted.

When the movie ended, he tipped up my chin

and kissed me. How could I have ever disliked this man? He was sweet, kind, and ultra-romantic. Or was it just a ruse so he could have a good vacation? When he went home to Florida, would he even remember me?

"I don't want to go back to the motel," he whispered. "But tomorrow is a workday, and it's after ten so I suppose we should lock up and leave, right?"

"I thought maybe we'd spend the night," I told him.

"I didn't bring my jammies," he teased.

"Neither did I."

He scooped me up like a bride—as if I weighed less than a feather pillow—and carried me up the stairs to my old bedroom. I'd forgotten how small that regular-sized bed was until he laid me down on it.

"Rocky, I'm not this person. I don't jump into relationships and go to bed with guys I've only known a few days," I whispered.

"I know, darlin'," he said softly. "But I'm sure glad you made an exception for me, especially when we got off to such a horrible start. You know, I think I was in love with you that night that you tripped me."

Chapter 12

Rocky had been in Jefferson for a whole week by that Friday. How could that be possible? He'd gone to show a local house that morning, and I was working on the agency website, removing the sold properties and putting in the four new ones we'd acquired that week when the bell above the door rang, and a woman walked in the front door. She wore a pair of skinny jeans and a skin-tight white cotton shirt. Long, dark hair fell into curls, floating on her shoulders, and her big blue eyes took in the whole place in a single glance. She folded her arms across her chest and tapped her foot as daggers shot through her eyes toward me.

I didn't even know the girl so it couldn't be me or something I'd done because I'd never even seen her before. "Good morning. What can I do for you?"

"I'm here to see Jessica Graham."

"Do you have an appointment?" I asked.

"I don't need an appointment. This is personal," she snapped.

"I see. I'm Jessica. Now what can I do for you, Miss…"

"Sabrina O'Dell. Is Rockwell still here?"

"Who?"

"Rockwell Rycroft?"

"Oh, you mean Rocky?" At first, I thought maybe she was his sister, but the woman I saw in the restaurant had much shorter hair than this one and her shoulders weren't as wide.

"Yes, I mean Rocky. God, I hate it when people call him that. It sounds like a nickname for a cartoon character. His name is Rockwell." Her chin shot up and she looked down her nose at me. "Of course, in a place like this, where everyone calls everyone else by stupid names, I suppose he'd be called Rocky. I'm here to tell you that it's time Rockwell comes home where he belongs. This hole in the road isn't his style. I don't know what hold you've got on him, but honey, it won't last long. He's played the field a few times before, but he always comes back to me." Her eyes danced with anger.

I imagined that mine were two-stepping with just as much anger as hers when I asked, "Are you his wife?"

"No, but I will be by Christmas. It's time for him to settle down. It was decided years ago that we would be together." Sabrina flipped her hair to one side. "I've been in Europe for a month. When I got home yesterday, Uncle Jake told me where he was and how it all started. This is his last fling, and now he's going to get married and make a good partner in the firm." Every word and gesture oozed confidence.

"You seem really sure of yourself," I said.

She pointed her finger at me and looked at me as if I was what she'd tracked in from a cow pasture. "Tell him Sabrina has been here. She's home from Europe. She'll be at the hotel in Tyler tonight and she's expecting him at seven."

"I'm not telling him jack squat. I am not your hired help." Each word got a little louder and a lot shriller.

"Oh, yes you will, or I'll track him down and tell him myself," she threatened.

I pulled a piece of business stationery from the desk drawer, wrote on it, and handed it to her. "He's showing a house at this address. And while you are there, could you ask him to pick up a dozen chocolate-chip cookies from the bakery? It will save me a trip."

Sabrina snatched the piece of paper right out of my hands. "Oh, honey, you're playing with the big dogs, and I don't think you can handle it."

"If a woman can't play with the big dogs, then

she'd better get off the porch, right?" I stood up, towering over her. "This happens to be my porch. I'm used to chasin' big, old bad bitches off my porch. So, chase your happy little butt on out to that address and see who wins today...honey."

"You are a big, dumb, blond bitch. Rocky won't even come back to get his belongings, let alone bring home cookies." Sabrina sniffed loudly as her high heels stomped across the floor, the effect lost in the plush carpet.

"One." I held up a finger.

"What?" Sabrina turned around.

"One time you get a warning for calling me a bitch. The second time you get your teeth rearranged. The third time there won't be a Sabrina left to hassle anyone else about Rocky."

"Don't threaten me," she hissed.

"No threats. Just solid cold facts. You got the warning. Now go see Rocky, and drive real easy on your way out of town. If you break one little speed-limit law, if you don't slow down for a stop sign or forget to wear your seat belt, you might end up in jail, and wouldn't it be a shame if there wasn't a lawyer in town to represent you or even a bail bondsman willing to get you out. Here in the backwoods, we take care of our own."

She slammed the door hard enough to rattle the paintings on the wall.

———————

I was still pacing the office floor and cussin' like a seasoned sailor when Ashley came into the office a few minutes later. "Good morning. I am not here to work but we are home. We had a wonderful time, and I'll be back to work on Monday."

"It's been a crazy morning." I told her all about the visit from Sabrina.

Ashley sat down in one of the chairs across from my desk and nodded at all the right places. "You should get into your truck and go to that property, drop down on the ground and kiss her feet. She has brought this whole thing to a head for you. Either he's serious or else it's over. You will know if it's a relationship or it was a fling."

"I don't want it to be over," I groaned.

"News flash, little sister." Ashley grinned. "Just before Danny proposed to me, there was another woman—a cute red-haired girl from up around Smithland. She came over here one Saturday night with a bunch of her girlfriends, looking for me. I got word that they were asking about me, so I found them and asked what the deal was. Same story. Different age. Different type. She said she'd been sleeping with him for a year and was going to mop up the streets of Jefferson with me if I didn't break it off with him." Ashley laughed.

I got up and paced around the room. "I never heard this before. What did you do?"

"Told Mama. She told me the same thing I just told you," Ashley said.

"But you weren't sleeping with Danny?" I groaned.

"Oh, yes, I was." Ashley giggled. "But I didn't tell Momma that. When I gave Danny a chance to explain, he admitted that he'd gone out with her three months before but had broken up with her to date me."

"What will I do if he goes with her?"

"Get over it," Ashley said. "That's the only option you have."

———

"Anybody home?" James popped the door open minutes after Ashley had left. "Jessie? Rocky? Where are you?"

"Back here," I yelled from the utility room where I was hunting down a roll of paper towels to clean up a cup of coffee I'd spilled. "James, is that you?"

"Where's Rocky?" He hiked a hip on the edge of the desk. "You've got fire in your eyes. I've got an hour before time to be in court. Spill it. I came by to tell you that I'm putting my house up for sale and looking for a place with maybe five or ten acres. You want to sell me the farm? But first tell me what's got your underbritches in a twist."

I wasn't sure my nerves could tell the story again, but it came tumbling out as I paced around the desk. James frowned and then laughed and then frowned again.

"You should've knocked her through the plateglass window. I would have defended you and gotten you off on the assault charge, and you'd have felt a lot better right now. Can we talk about my house, or do we need to discuss this some more?" he asked.

I sat down behind my desk. "Why are you putting your house on the market? You've loved that little cottage ever since you bought it two years ago."

"Because I want something bigger and with more kitchen room," he said.

"Colleen?" It was good to think about something other than whether Rocky would just come back to tell me that it was over.

James blushed. "It will take a while to sell my

place and probably even longer to buy something but, yes, Colleen. And don't fuss at me. I really, really feel chemistry with her, Jessie. I think this could go somewhere, and if it does, I want to be ready."

"I'm happy for you." I meant it. James deserved someone that made him happy. I only hoped that I could be so lucky.

"Time's up, darlin'. I've got to go to court. If the hussy comes back, kick her all the way to the street, and then call me while she's dialin' 911." He grinned.

I stood in the window, watching cars go by, replaying the past week through my mind, one frame at a time. It was probably only a few minutes, but it seemed like hours before Rocky's truck pulled up in the parking lot. He sat there for a long time, and I figured he'd come to say goodbye.

Finally, he got out of the truck, and I hurried back to my desk. I backed up and sat on the edge for support as I watched him slowly walk up the sidewalk, pause at the door, and hesitate several moments before he turned the knob. He looked at the carpet when he entered the room and my heart stopped.

He finally looked into my eyes. "Guess I'd better do some tall talking."

I nodded very slowly and asked, "Where's Sabrina?"

"Gone home. Gone to Dallas. Gone to Europe again. Gone to hell for all I care," he said with a long sigh.

My heart sounded like a bass drum thumping in my ears. "And what are you going to do?"

"Depends on you, I guess," Rocky said.

"Well, I intend to fight for what we've got. I happen to be in love with you. I even like you. And that's important. If we're ever going to have a permanent relationship out on that farm, it's essential that I like you as well as love you. And I do both. Sabrina might think she's got you tied to a way of life, but I intend to show you something different. So now what are you going to do?"

"I'm sorry that she came here and tried to stir up trouble," he said.

"The past is the past. It's gone and can't be called up to be redone. What's important is right now. I love you. It's too soon for either of us to say that but I do."

He was around the desk in two easy, long-legged strides and gathered me into his arms. "I love you, Jessica Graham. With my whole heart and all that I am, I love you."

Chapter 13

I COULD HARDLY WAIT FOR FRIDAYS TO COME TO an end so I could drive over the border to Shreveport, Louisiana. That was the closest airport, and Rocky flew in to spend every weekend that he could with me. He wanted to rent a car, but if I met him at the airport, that meant I got an extra hour with him on Friday and on Sunday evening when I took him back. We were making a long-distance relationship work with video chats every night, dozens of texts through the day, and weekends together.

"We've got the week wrapped up." Ashley came out of her office and poured a glass of sweet tea. "You can go if you want to."

"His plane doesn't land until seven, so I'd just walk the floor and watch the clock. I'll stay but you can leave if you want."

She sank down in a chair. "My guys are having a tailgate party at the football game tonight. Graham can't wait until next year when he gets to suit up with the high school team. All I hear about at home is quarterbacks, plays, and fumbles. You have got to get married soon and have a daughter so we can talk shoes, shopping, and makeup."

"Why don't you and Danny have a tagalong? You're only thirty-eight. That's the new twenty-five, you know."

"Don't tempt me." Ashley smiled. "But I'll leave the girls up to you and Rocky. You think Edward will ever come around?"

"Probably not but I'm okay with that. I got my second wish to meet my father, and it brought me the love of my life so I can't complain. Sometimes fate or destiny or God, whatever it is, works in mysterious ways. If I hadn't gone looking for Edward, I would have never found Rocky."

"Life is a crazy ride, isn't it?" Ashley pointed to the clock on the wall. "Ten, nine, eight, seven, six, five, four, three, two, one—now it's officially five o'clock and time to go home. Have a great weekend. And remember, we're all going out to eat after church on Sunday at the Italian place."

"We'll be there." I gathered up my purse and tote bag, gave my sister a hug, and headed out the door. Leaves had begun to drop from the two oak trees in the parking lot. Fall was pushing out summer a day at a time. It wouldn't be long until Rocky and I would spend our first Christmas together.

I thought about what kind of gifts I'd get for him as I drove toward Shreveport. It only took an hour on a good day to go from Jefferson to Shreveport, but the interstate could get pretty busy at five o'clock on Friday. If I arrived too early, I could always wait for him in baggage claim.

There was a holdup right near the Louisiana border over a little fender bender, and I sat in line for fifteen minutes while they got the two vehicles off the road. To pass the time, I read through the texts that Rocky had sent throughout the day. Some of them made me giggle; most of them still turned my cheeks crimson. When I finally made it to the airport, I had to circle through the parking garage three times before I finally found a space. I rushed inside to find him waiting for his suitcase to come around the conveyor belt at the baggage claim.

"Hey." He opened his arms.

I walked into them and breathed in the scent of his aftershave. When he kissed me, I tasted peanuts and coffee. "I missed you so much. The weeks get longer every time I have to be away from you."

His suitcase finally came around and he grabbed it. Carrying it in one hand, he laced his fingers in mine with the other one as we made our way out of the terminal. When we reached my truck, I handed him the keys. He put his suitcase in the back and then wrapped me in his arms for a long, hard kiss. "It's not ever going to get any closer between the two places."

Traffic was light so we made it to the farmhouse in a little over an hour. Callie met us at the door, and the smell of soup simmering in a slow cooker filled the air. Rocky parked his suitcase at the bottom of the stairs, stopped long enough to scratch Callie's ears, and then swept me up into his arms. His lips found mine in one scorching-hot kiss after another as he carried me up to my old bedroom.

It was fully dark when we made it back down to the kitchen, and we'd both worked up a ferocious appetite. We were sitting at the table when he covered my hand with his. "I've looked forward to this all week, darlin'. I brought something for you but right now let's just eat and talk about the future."

"You talk. I'll listen."

"I'll start with a question," he said. "Number one." He held up one finger.

"I thought you said 'a question,'" I said.

"Several," he said.

"Okay." I was hoping that he'd ask *the question*, but I guess it was too early after only six weeks.

"Number one. I will be talking to a banker tomorrow morning about a new job. I sent him my résumé this week, and he's impressed with it. If he hires me, and I take the job, I'll be working as a loan officer, dealing with real estate primarily."

"Is that a question?" Why would he be changing jobs, only to work in basically the same field but with less money?

"No, but this is. The job is at one of the banks here in Jefferson. Do you have a problem with me living here at the farmhouse with you and Callie?"

"Oh. My. Goodness!" I squealed and threw myself into his arms, showering him with kisses. "Please tell me you are serious. Don't be teasing me."

"I'm not teasing, and I've never been more serious about anything in my whole life," Rocky said, "but you didn't answer my question. Can I move in with you?"

"Yes! Yes! A thousand times yes!" I sat down in his lap and kissed him until we were both breathless.

"Question number two?" He panted.

"Whatever it is, the answer is yes." I nodded.

He reached into his pants pocket and brought out a velvet box. My heart stopped. I don't mean that it skipped a beat—it stopped dead. My hands went clammy. My pulse raced and I couldn't stop staring at that beautiful red box.

"Jessica Susanne Graham, will you marry me?" He snapped it open to reveal a sparkling engagement ring.

I was so speechless that for several seconds all I could do was nod.

"Does that mean the answer to question number two is still yes?" he asked.

"Yes, yes, yes!" I found my voice.

He slipped the ring on my finger, and I wrapped my arms around his neck, keeping the sparkling diamonds in plain view so that I could still see them glistening in the light. I was marrying my soul mate, and maybe by this time next year, I'd even have that baby girl that Ashley wanted in the family.

I couldn't say a word for several minutes. I was almost too excited to eat supper. Food was my answer for everything from sorrow to joy.

When we finally had the cleanup done and were

cuddled up on the sofa trying to decide on a date for a wedding, he suddenly stood up and headed out to the foyer.

"Leaving me so soon?" I teased.

"No, I remembered that I brought something for you." He unzipped the side pocket of his suitcase.

"I thought this gorgeous ring was what you brought me." I held it up to the light, still wondering if I was dreaming.

"It's a double prize night." He put an envelope in my hands that had my name on the outside. No return. No stamp but the writing looked very familiar.

"What's this?" I asked.

"Don't know. I'm just the messenger." He sat down beside me and draped his arm around my shoulders. "But you might want to read it."

I held the letter in my hands long after I'd recognized the handwriting from Edward's letters to my mother. When I was eight years old and made the wish that I would meet my father, I would have squealed to have a letter from my father, but tonight with Rocky's proposal, the letter took a back seat to what was most important in my life.

"Well?" Rocky asked.

I dropped it in my lap and laid my head on his shoulder. "I don't know if I want to know what it says. Maybe I'll just put it up for a few years."

"Aren't you even a little curious?" he asked.

I barely nodded. "Of course I am, but this night is so special that I don't want to ruin it."

"Want me to read it to you?" He asked.

"No, but hold me, please. And don't argue with me if I tear it into shreds after I read the thing." I slowly opened the envelope and closed my eyes as I unfolded it. Then I took a very deep breath and read:

Dear Jessica,

I'm not sure how to begin to write this letter. You have been on my mind so often these past weeks. I've talked it over with my wife, Eva. Mainly because I believe that she needs to be informed and willing for what I want to do. And she's stood beside me faithfully.

I loved your mother with a love that can't be described in words. It was something neither of us seemed to have control over, as you've already read in those letters. That anyone else would ever know how I felt about her and she, me, is more than a little bit embarrassing.

I would like very much to get to know you, and Eva has agreed. I think it would be best if we started off as friends and see what can develop from that. Rocky talks about you so much I feel like I already know a lot about you...but I'd like to spend some time with you. If you'd even consider such a notion, please let me know. Awaiting your answer.

Edward Rollin

It was so much more formal than the carefree letters that he'd written to my mother, but then they'd known each other intimately. With mixed emotions I laid the letter on the end table.

"Well?" Rocky said.

"He wants to be my friend," I said. "I just realized that since Tamara is married to your brother, she's going to be my sister-in-law as well as my half sister when we get married."

Rocky laughed. "That's hardly what I expected you to say."

"I'm not sure how I feel about his offer so I'm

going to think about it a few days before I call him with an answer. But I do know how I feel about you, darlin', and our engagement and upcoming marriage. I know beyond a shadow of a doubt that I love you and I'm so glad that I went to Florida. Now let's go back upstairs and take a long shower together. What's important right now is us, and I want to spend the whole night celebrating that."

"Yes, ma'am." Rocky took my hand and together we went back to the bedroom.

Chapter 14

ASHLEY STEPPED UP ON A CHAIR TO PUT THE VEIL on my head on that second Saturday evening in December. The idea that I was marrying Rocky was surreal even though my sister and I had planned the wedding for three months.

"Wow!" Danny peeked inside the nursery where I was getting dressed and then came on inside. "I'm looking at the two most stunning women in the whole state of Texas. Ashley, darlin', you should wear red velvet more often. And poor old Rocky is going to be speechless when he sees you in that."

"I have something to say before we do this." I swallowed hard several times before the lump in my throat disappeared. "You both have always been there for me. Ashley has been as much mother as sister, and I couldn't ask for a better brother than you've been all these years, Danny. You've both been my rock."

"Right back atcha kid." Danny said hoarsely as

he held out his hand to help Ashley down from the chair.

She grabbed a tissue and dabbed at her eyes. "You're going to make me cry, and we agreed not to get all sentimental today. Mama wouldn't want that."

"Your man of honor is here." James breezed into the room. He looked taller somehow in his black tux with the red cummerbund and tie that matched Ashley's dress. "Thank you for picking red and for not expecting me to carry a bouquet."

I handed him a white velvet pillow with our wedding rings tied in the middle with a satin ribbon. "No problem. I love it that you are the ring bearer as well as bridesmaid."

"When I marry Colleen, I will expect the same from you," he said.

"My pleasure," I told him as Ashley put a dozen red roses in my arms. "And when will that be?"

"Before summer, maybe at Valentine's. If you get a holiday wedding, then I should get one, too. There's the music. Time for us to go, Ashley. I love you, Jessie. Be happy."

"Love all of you. Have you seen Rocky?" I whispered as I looped my arm into Danny's. "Ashley wouldn't even let me talk to him. Made me stay at her house last night and all day today. We should have run off to Jamaica and not told a living soul until it was all done."

Danny and I proceeded to the double doors that led from the church foyer into the sanctuary. "I saw Rocky a few minutes ago, and he's every bit as nervous as you are. His sister, who is his best woman, is knock-down-dead good-looking, and I bet all the men at the reception forget about the tall, beautiful bride when they see her. Rocky's uncle Jasper is a hoot and is real proud to be his groomsman. It's time. You look lovely. Now let's go get this part done so we can go to the party. I know you're hungry."

"Starving," I admitted honestly as the doors opened.

From the moment I could see Rocky standing up there with his sister beside him and his uncle Jasper on the other side of her, all my jitters disappeared. In a few minutes I would be Mrs. Rocky Rycroft. He gave me the whole package—sparks, electricity, and chemistry—and I was getting it for the rest of my life.

The preacher made a motion with his hands, and everyone rose to their feet. I could hear the shuffling and the sweet comments about my dress as I walked past friends and family, but nothing mattered except making it to the pulpit where Rocky waited. Ashley stepped up to take my bouquet, and Danny put my hands into Rocky's and stepped back to sit on the front pew with Trey and Graham.

"Who gives this woman to be married to this man?" the preacher asked.

"I do," Ashley said from her place.

He went on to do the ceremony. "Rocky and Jessica, I'm honored to have been asked to perform this ceremony. I've watched Jessica grow up from a baby. I christened her at birth, and her mother was faithful in bringing both of her daughters to church every week, so it's with pleasure that I share this special day with you both. I'd like to speak to you about a passage of scripture found in the thirteenth chapter of First Corinthians. It says there that love is kind, love isn't jealous."

Ashley wiped a tear and James sniffled.

"Love knows no boundaries," the preacher said. I really was trying to listen, but Rocky's eyes met mine, and we were in our own world.

"Rocky, do you take this woman to be your wife?" the preacher asked.

Rocky pulled me toward him and kissed me on the forehead. "I take you to be my wife, Jessica. I want to live with you through hardships and good times. I want to come home with you at night to know the love and comfort in your arms. I promise to be faithful for all our life together, and I promise to love, keep, and protect this love between us with a jealous zeal all the days of my life."

"Jessica, do you take Rocky to be your husband?"

After that, I wasn't sure I could get words out without crying. "I will be your helpmeet through bad times as well as good ones. I promise to be faithful until my last breath, and I promise to never forsake this love we have between us or take it for granted. I will love you up to and through all eternity."

We exchanged rings. His was a wide gold band and mine matched my engagement ring. The preacher said a brief prayer and pronounced us man and wife, Mr. and Mrs. Rocky Rycroft.

The reception was held in the church fellowship hall. Ashley, Rocky's sister, Christine, and his mother, Marlene, had joined forces two days before and decorated it with poinsettias and Christmas decorations in every corner. After we took pictures with the cake and had our first glass of wedding punch together, Ashley nodded toward Graham, who oversaw music.

Rocky led me out to the middle of the reception room floor as Blake Shelton's voice filled the room with "God Gave Me You." We'd danced together before in the living room at the farmhouse but tonight was special. The lyrics talked about staying in this moment for the rest of time and not missing a thing. I intended to live the rest of my life with that motto. Each minute that we spent together would be something precious, and I'd work at not taking it for granted, just like I had said in my vows.

There would be tough times. We were both too volatile and hot-tempered to expect there would never be a fight or an argument. We'd already weathered several in the past few months, but as long as he could take me in his arms and two-step across the foyer with me, or take me upstairs to our bedroom, we could make it work.

Everyone clapped when the song ended, and the DJ struck up a livelier country western tune. Several other couples took the dance floor, and Rocky and I were on the way to the head table when Edward touched me on the shoulder.

"You are a beautiful bride," he said. "Congratulations to you and Rocky both."

"I'm glad you are here. It's customary for the father to dance with the bride but if you aren't comfortable with that, I understand." I said.

He held out his hand and I took it. I'd come prepared—just in case—so I nodded toward Graham. It might not be a traditional one, but then we weren't a typical father and daughter. The Cajun beat of the fiddles echoed off the walls with Mary Chapin Carpenter's "Twist and Shout." In some ways, it was a tribute to Mama's Louisiana roots, in others, I chose it because she loved upbeat music.

"I was expecting something sentimental," Edward said. "But let's give 'em something to talk about, Jessica."

My father almost put me to shame with his dance moves, and before it was over, I'd crooked my finger to invite Tamara to join us and the three of us put on a show for the folks. When the song ended, Tamara grabbed me and Edward in a three-way hug. It was the first time he'd ever shown emotion toward me and the first time that I felt a stirring in my heart for him.

There was an awkward moment when we all

stepped away from each other. Then Rocky laced his fingers in mine and led me toward the head table. Before we got there, Eva tapped me on the shoulder. "Thank you for inviting us. We hope that maybe you'll make time for a few hours at Christmas. It would mean the world to Tamara—and to Edward and me."

"Thank you," Rocky said.

I nodded. "We'd love to."

"We'll take all of this a baby step at a time," he whispered.

"That's the only way I can handle it," I told him.

It was ten o'clock when we finally got away. Everyone threw rice at us as we drove off in Rocky's truck. When we reached the farmhouse, he carried me over the threshold—our honeymoon place since he didn't have time to take off from his new job at the bank. I kicked my satin shoes off and turned around for him to unzip my dress. When he finished, I stepped out of it and let it puddle up on the floor at the bottom of the staircase.

"I love you." He scooped me up in my lacy white underwear, my veil trailing along on the floor behind us as he climbed the steps.

"This has been the best day of my whole life.

The third wish has been granted." I said as he laid me on our brand-new king-sized bed.

"Third wish?" he asked.

"When I was a little girl, I found a bottle on the beach and made three wishes. One was that I would find a conch shell. The second one was that I'd meet my father. And the third was that someday I'd find my true love and live happily ever after. Today my third wish came true."

"Yes, it did." He stretched out beside me and wrapped the veil around both of us, creating a cocoon for only Mr. and Mrs. Rocky Rycroft.

If you love Carolyn Brown's contemporary romance, read on for a look at beloved author Sharon Sala's latest

NEW YORK TIMES AND USA TODAY BESTSELLING AUTHOR

SHARON SALA

THE NEXT BEST DAY

Available November 2022 from Sourcebooks Casablanca

Chapter 1

IT WAS SATURDAY IN ALBUQUERQUE. THE FIRST Saturday in February and it was cold. But weather was not an issue for twenty-nine-year-old Katie McGrath. She awakened in a state of absolute bliss, calm and confident in everything this day would bring, because she was getting married.

And she wasn't just gaining a husband. She was getting a family, something she'd never had. She didn't know where she came from, or who her parents were, or if she had any extended family. All she'd ever known was foster care.

She'd come close to getting adopted more than once, but every time, something would happen. Either the couple changed their minds about adopting or decided she wasn't the right fit for their family.

By the time she was twelve, she had a chip on her shoulder and was tired of pretending anyone cared about her. At that point, she was just another half-grown kid in the foster care system, so she made her peace with it and finally aged out.

Once she graduated from high school in Chicago and left the foster care system, she knew exactly what she was going to do. She wanted to be a teacher, and with the help of a couple of grants and working two jobs for four years, she put herself through college.

Coming to Albuquerque to teach, which was where she was now, was also where she met Mark Roman. He was a farm boy from Kansas who had a junior position in a CPA firm, while Katie taught at Saguaro Elementary. Now, three years later, here they were, ready to take that next step in their relationship, and she couldn't be happier.

She was just getting out of the shower when she got a text from Lila Reece, a fellow teacher who'd become her best friend, and today, her maid of honor.

It was a "good morning, good luck, see you at the chapel" kind of message, but it brought reality to the day. It was time to get moving.

After breakfast, Katie loaded up her things, made a quick trip to her hairdresser, then hurried off to the chapel to meet Lila.

Lila was short, blond, and curvy—the opposite of Katie, who was tall with dark shoulder-length hair and the metabolism Lila longed for.

When Katie pulled up in the parking lot, Lila helped carry in the dress and everything that went with it.

"I love your hair!" Lila said, eyeing the smooth, silky strands as they headed inside.

Katie smiled. "Thanks. This style works really well with the veil," she said.

They spent the next couple of hours getting ready in one of the dressing rooms, laughing and talking.

Gordy Thurman, Mark's best man, arrived early, too, and popped in to give her a thumbs-up.

"Hey, Katie, you look beautiful. So do you, Lila," he said.

"Thanks," Katie said. "Is Mark here yet?"

"Not yet, but we both know Mark Roman is never going to be the early bird. He'll be here soon," Gordy said, then waved and went to find the men's dressing room.

The wedding chapel was a popular venue, even though the wedding wasn't going to be a large one.

Just Katie and Mark.

A maid of honor and a best man…and fifty guests.

The florist stopped by the bride's dressing room to drop off flowers, then scurried away.

Katie was listening without comment to Lila's continuous spiel about what a fun weeklong honeymoon she and Mark were going to have at the Bellagio hotel in Vegas.

"You're going to be in the honeymoon suite, living it up. That should warrant enough good luck to do a little gambling while you're there," Lila said.

Katie laughed. "We have a little money put aside for that, too."

They were down to finishing touches when Katie finally sat on a bench so that Lila could fasten the veil to Katie's hair.

Once Lila finished, she eyed the pretty woman before her and sighed.

"You look breathtaking, my friend. Your wedding dress is as elegant as you are. Mark is one very lucky man."

Katie shivered. "I'm the lucky one," she said, then got up, moved to the full-length mirror in the corner of the room, and did a full turn, eyeing herself from front to back. She felt beautiful and loved.

She was still thinking of Mark when her cell phone rang. When she saw it was him, joy bubbled up into her voice.

"Hello, darling. Are you as ready as I am?"

"Um…Katie…I have something to tell you," Mark said.

Katie laughed. "Sorry, but last-minute jitters are not allowed."

"It's not jitters, Katie. I'm so sorry, but I can't marry you."

Katie's knees went out from under her. For a few horror-filled moments, this was her childhood all over again. She reached backward for a chair that wasn't there and sat down on the floor.

"What do you mean, you can't marry me?"

Lila saw her fall and then heard those words coming out of Katie's mouth and gasped, but when she started toward her, Katie held up her hand.

Lila froze in midstep—horrified.

"I can't marry you, because I'm already married…to Megan. We eloped to Vegas last night. I'm sorry but—"

Katie went numb. "Megan who?" Then she gasped. "Megan, your boss's daughter, Megan? You married Walt Lanier's daughter? Just like that?"

Mark Roman sighed. "No, not just like that. We've been seeing each other for a while and—"

Katie's voice rose two octaves. "You've been cheating on me and still playing out this wedding lie? When you knew it wasn't going to happen? What kind of a lowlife does that?"

"I know you're—"

Katie interrupted him again. "Oh! Now your unexpected promotion makes sense. Your boss can't have his daughter married to a lowly CPA in the financial department."

"Look, Katie. I'm sorry. I didn't mean to hurt you. It just—"

Tears were rolling down Katie's face, and her heart was pounding so hard she didn't know she was screaming.

"You lie! You don't give a damn about what you just did to me. Just stop talking. I can't believe I was this blind, but I'm beginning to realize how freaking lucky I am to find this out about you now. You are a cheat and a liar, and you just sold your honor and your word for money. You deserve each other."

"I'm sorry… I'm really—"

Katie interrupted him again.

"Not as sorry as you're going to be when you

remember everything about today was paid for with your credit card," Katie said, and hung up.

Lila's eyes were wide with unshed tears, and she kept staring at Katie, waiting for the explanation.

Katie looked up. "Mark married his boss's daughter last night. They eloped to Vegas. Our Vegas. Will you help me up? I have to tell the guests."

Lila reached for Katie with both arms and pulled her up and then hugged her so hard.

"I'm so sorry, Katie. I'm stunned. I can't believe he just—"

Katie pushed Lila away and took a deep breath.

"I should have known. I should have known. I have never been enough," she mumbled. "God give me strength."

Then she tore off the veil, tossed it aside, yanked up the front of her skirt with both hands so she wouldn't trip, and strode out of the dressing room.

Gordy had just received the same phone call from Mark and was coming to look for Katie when he saw her storming up the hall toward the sanctuary with Lila running behind her, trying to catch up.

"Katie, I don't know what to—"

She just shook her head and kept walking,

unaware Gordy and Lila were behind her. They stopped at the door to the sanctuary, but Katie kept walking down the aisle before stopping at the pulpit and turning around to face the guests.

Her eyes were red and tear-filled, and the splotches on her cheeks were obvious signs she'd been crying. Total humiliation was imminent, but she lifted her chin and met their gaze.

"I have just been informed there will be no wedding today. I'm not getting married. Mark eloped with his boss's daughter last night. They got married in Vegas. Thank you for coming. Please take your gifts home with you when you leave. The wedding food will be going to a homeless shelter."

The communal gasp was so loud Katie felt like it sucked the air from the room, and then the buzzing undertone of shocked whispers began.

She went back up the aisle with her chin up and her head back.

"Worst day of my life," she muttered, and walked back to the dressing room and changed into the clothes she'd arrived in. She left the wedding dress and shoes in a pile on the floor, leaving Lila to contact the caterers to have them pack up the food and take it to a shelter.

Lila kept telling her not to worry, she'd take care of everything and call her tonight, but all Katie could do was thank her and hug her.

She couldn't face the pity.

She couldn't face herself.

She wasn't enough.

She drove home in a daze.

———

Meanwhile, Mark Roman was alternating between being a happy bridegroom and feeling like an asshole, which was fair because he qualified in both categories. When he'd told Megan he had to make the call to Katie and needed some privacy, she'd been more than understanding.

"I totally understand, darling. I have some things to take care of anyway. I'll be back later," she said.

So now he'd made the dreaded call and Megan was still gone, and he was too rattled to go looking for her, which, as it turned out, was for the best because Megan was only two floors down in one of the suites reserved for the big spenders the casinos called whales.

And this particular whale, who went by the name of Craig Buttoni, didn't just gamble with money. He was in the drug game up to his eyeballs, and Megan and her father, Walt, were, in a sense, his employees.

Walt Lanier used his CPA business as a front, while he controlled the flow of cocaine coming in and going out of New Mexico. From time to time, Megan had her own little part in the business, and she'd just fucked it up by getting married to an outsider.

Craig Buttoni was pissed, and when he found out she was honeymooning in Vegas, he sent her a text she couldn't refuse, demanding her presence in his suite.

The moment she knocked on his door, he opened it, grabbed her hand long enough to look at the size of the ring on her hand, rolled his eyes, and then pulled her into his suite and locked the door.

"Is he making payments on that thing?"

Megan glared. Buttoni was in his late forties, with a bulldog underbite and diamonds in his ears. His eyes were always at half-squint, and she was just a little bit scared of him. She didn't like the comment or the tone of his voice, and snatched her hand back.

"I didn't see you offering anything better," she snapped. "I'm happy. Be happy for me."

Craig liked it when she got feisty, but business was business.

"He's not in the loop. He could cause us trouble," Craig said.

Megan glared. "You keep your hands off him. If I think he's dangerous to us, I'll just dump him. I got married in Vegas. I can get unmarried here if the need arises."

Craig held up his hands and took a step backward.

"There's a lot riding on your itch for sex. Just making sure we understand each other," he said.

"I can scratch my own itch," Megan said. "I married him because I love him."

Craig threw back his head and laughed. "Okay. But you're the one with the most to lose. He can't suspect anything. If you fuck up, you know my rule for fuckups."

"Yes. You eliminate them," Megan muttered. "I'm leaving now. Happy roll of the dice," she said, and let herself out.

When Megan got back to the honeymoon suite and saw the look on Mark's face, she knew what she had to do, and it all revolved around getting naked.

———

Katie holed up in her apartment for the entire week that would have been her honeymoon. She slept away the shock, then ate away the rage, and ignored the phone calls from everyone but Lila. Those she took, only to reassure her best friend that she was still kicking. By the time she was ready to go back to Saguaro Elementary, she had her game face on.

It took that week of solitude to remind herself that, in the grand scheme of things, her heart had been broken, but nobody died. She was tougher than some man's lies. She didn't need a man to take care of her. She didn't need anyone. Ever again.

It was time to go back to work. Some would talk behind her back. And some would not. But her first-grade students would not know the depth of her heartbreak. She'd been Miss Katie before and she was still Miss Katie. She would keep their little world safe and secure, and they would know they were loved.

For Katie, it was enough.

———

Six weeks later

Katie was getting ready to walk her class down to the cafeteria for lunch.

"Boys and girls, if you brought your lunch, get it out of your backpack and get in line," she said, and then took a deep breath when two of her six-year-olds suddenly lost their minds, launched at each other, and began wrestling on the floor. "Oh no! Alejandro! Kieran! I'm so sorry, but you forgot the rules. Get up and go to the back of the line."

Alejandro scrambled to his feet, his dark eyes wide with instant distress.

"But, Miss Katie, it's my turn to be leader!" he said.

"I know!" Katie said, keeping the tone of her voice between regret and it's out of my hands. "You and Kieran made bad choices. Now, get to the back of the line and do not look at each other. Do not touch each other. And just to make sure, I'll be watching you to help you not forget again. Allison, you will be leader today."

"Yes, ma'am," the little girl said, and strode to the front of the line like she was walking a runway.

Katie sighed again. Three more hours and Saguaro Elementary would be out for spring break. It was none too soon.

The past weeks had been stressful beyond words. By the time she'd returned to work, everyone knew what had happened. Half of the staff wanted to talk about it. The other half just gave her sad, hangdog looks. It was the students who'd saved her sanity. They didn't know what had happened, and the few who'd asked her if her name had changed were fine when she answered, "No."

But today, the kids were antsy to be gone, too, and Alejandro and Kieran were examples of the lack of focus within the building.

Katie glanced up at the clock again, then nodded at Allison.

"It's time. Lead the way," Katie said, and watched Allison disappear out the door, with the other students in line behind her. Katie stayed toward the back of the line to make sure her little rebels were still there, and up the hall they went.

They were halfway to the cafeteria when they began hearing popping sounds and what sounded like a scream in another part of the building.

Before she could get on her walkie to check in with the office, the principal was on the school intercom, and the tremble in her voice was enough to freeze Katie's blood.

"We have an active shooter in the building. Proceed with lockdown procedures immediately."

Katie groaned. She was halfway between her

room and the lunchroom so she immediately ran to the nearest classroom, which happened to be Lila's room, and yanked the door open.

Lila was already in lockdown mode and running to lock the door when Katie appeared.

"Lila! We need to shelter with you. We were on our way to the cafeteria. It's too far from our classroom to go back!"

"Get them in here," Lila said, even as she was getting her students on the floor against the far wall, away from the door.

"In here! In here!" Katie cried, and began hurrying her students into the room.

A series of single shots rang out, as if the shooter was picking targets, but the screams she'd been hearing suddenly stopped, and the silence was more terrifying than the screams.

Katie was counting kids as they entered the room, and then realized she was missing two. In a panic, she spun and saw Alejandro back down the hall, lying on the floor with blood pouring from his nose, and Kieran kneeling beside him.

"Oh no," she groaned. "Lila. Proceed with lockdown. I've got two missing," she cried, and turned and ran.

Lila saw the little boys way down the hall, and Katie running in an all-out sprint to get to them, even as the screams and gunshots were getting louder.

"Hurry, Katie! Hurry!" Lila shouted, and then slammed the door shut and locked it before running back to the students who were now in a state of panic. Some were crying, and some were too scared to move. She had to get them into the safest part of the room and flat on their stomachs. The smaller the target, the harder they were to hit.

For Katie, the slamming door was a relief to hear. Her students were safe. Now all she had to do was get the last two and bring them inside with the rest of her class before it was too late.

—————

Alejandro was crying so loudly that he didn't hear his teacher calling to them, but Kieran did. When he heard Katie shouting at them, he looked up and realized the other kids were gone and the hall was empty.

"Get up, Alejandro! Miss Katie said we have to run!" Kieran cried.

At that point Alejandro looked up and realized they'd been left behind.

"Miss Katie…I fell!" he cried as Katie came to a sliding halt in front of them.

"I see, baby, I see," Katie said. "But we have to run now," she said, and grabbed them both by their hands and started back up the hall with them, moving as fast as their legs would take them.

All of a sudden, she heard the sound of running footsteps behind her and panicked.

Oh God, oh God…he's behind us. No time to get into another room. No time. No time.

And then some older students flew past her unattended.

"He got in our room. He shot our teacher," one girl cried as she flew past.

Katie got a firmer grip on the boys and began pulling them as she ran, but the shots were louder now. The shooter was getting closer.

Then out of nowhere, one of the coaches appeared at Katie's side. Their gazes met as he reached down to help her. His hand was on Kieran when a bullet hit him in the back of the head, splattering blood everywhere as he dropped.

Both boys screamed.

"Miss Katie!" Alejandro cried.

The shock of what Kieran had seen was too much as his little legs went out from under him.

Katie yanked Kieran up into her arms and pushed Alejandro in front of her.

"Run, baby, run!" she shouted. "Go to Miss Lila's room. See the door up ahead! Just run!"

No sooner had she said that when a bullet hit the floor between her feet, and then a second one ripped through her shoulder. It was like being stabbed with fire. She screamed, nearly dropping Kieran, and in a last-ditch effort to save the boys, she grabbed Alejandro and threw herself on top of them.

Kieran was screaming and Alejandro was in shock.

Katie's shoulder was on fire and everything was fading around her.

God, oh God, please don't let them die. She wrapped her arms around the both of them and held them close, whispering.

"Alejandro...Kieran. Don't talk. Don't move. I love you."

More gunshots rang out. She heard a body drop beside her, but she wouldn't look. Couldn't look.

And then there were more screams, more shots as Katie took a second shot in her back and everything went black.

Seconds later, police appeared in the hall in front of them and took the shooter down, but the damage was done. Katie was unconscious and bleeding out all over the boys beneath her.

———————

The shooting was all over the news, both locally and nationally.

Thirty-six hours later, of the five adults who had been shot, Katie McGrath was the only one still alive.

One student, a fifth-grade girl, died at the scene, and twelve other students had been shot and transported to hospitals. All but two of the surviving wounded were released within a couple of days, and the last two were due to go home tomorrow.

Only Katie's condition was unknown. Her tenuous hold on life was still wavering, and she had yet to wake up.

———————

Four days later

The news was traveling fast throughout the hospital.

Katie McGrath was exhibiting signs of regaining consciousness.

Lila Reece was all the "next of kin" Katie had, and she was on her way to the hospital for her daily visit when she got the call.

She cried the rest of the way there out of relief.

Visiting time was in progress when Lila entered the ICU. She went straight to the nurse's desk to get the update.

"Her heart rate is stronger. Her pulse is steady, and all of her vital signs show signs of waking," the nurse said.

Lila nodded, too emotional to comment, then hurried to Katie's bedside. She clasped Katie's hand and began patting it and rubbing it until she got herself together enough to speak.

"Hey, Katie, honey... It's me, Lila. Can you hear me? You have no idea how many people have been praying for you. Your students have been calling me every day, asking for updates. You saved them. They love you so much. We all do. I'm here. Right here. Nothing to be afraid of anymore."

Katie was trying to wake up, but she couldn't think what to do, or how to move. She heard a familiar voice and was struggling to focus on the words, but they were garbled.

Then she heard her name. Katie! Someone was calling her. She wanted to respond, but it was too hard, so she slid back into the quiet. But the voice wouldn't let her go.

Memories were coming back with the sounds. She'd been running. There was blood. *My students! Where are they?*

She moaned, then someone was holding her hand. She tried to grip the fingers, but moving made everything hurt.

The voice…familiar, but she kept trying to remember what happened.

We were running. Hide. Hide. Hide.

***

"Her eyelids are fluttering," Lila said.

The nurse nodded.

Lila leaned down near Katie's ear, speaking quietly.

"It's me, Katie. It's Lila. You were so strong for

the little ones. They're safe, Katie. They're all safe…and so are you."

A tear ran down the side of Katie's temple.

Lila's eyes welled. "You hear me. I know you hear me."

It took a few seconds for Lila to realize Katie was squeezing her fingers. Ecstatic, she squeezed back.

"Yes, Katie, yes, I'm here. I have to leave now, but I'll be back. You aren't alone, baby. You are not alone."

———

Visiting time was over and the floor was still bustling with nurses tending patients and doctors coming and going.

Katie's imminent awakening brought her surgeon to the ICU to check her stats, and someone had tipped off the media. They were back out in the hospital parking lot, waiting for her doctor to come out and make a statement regarding her status, because Katie McGrath's welfare had become the city's concern.

Video from the halls of Saguaro Elementary had shown the panic and horror of that day. There were images of teachers and children being shot on the run, and of the shooter coming out of classrooms he'd just shot up.

Parents were traumatized as they watched their children all running for their lives. And then the blessed relief of the arrival of the police, and the shooter being taken down.

The first funeral had come and gone, and three other funerals were imminent for victims. The grief and horror in the city were real.

There was a clip of Katie throwing herself on top of two little boys, and then getting shot in the back, that someone had leaked to the media. It was viewed tens of thousands of times before the administration realized and had it pulled.

The shooter was unknown to the community —a loner who'd been in Albuquerque only three months, and while the authorities were still investigating, his reason for what he'd done had died with him.

There were so many people grieving the people who'd died, and others coping with wounded children who were going to suffer lasting trauma to their bodies, and both teachers and children were so traumatized by the incident they didn't want to go back to school. They all needed good news, and finding out that Katie McGrath might be waking up was it.

───────

Katie opened her eyes to a nurse and a doctor standing at her bedside.

She recognized being in a hospital, but she was confused about why. She hurt. Had she been in a wreck? What had—?

And then it hit her! The shooting!

"The boys…the boys…" Her voice drifted off, but the doctor knew what she meant.

"Your students are safe. The two little boys you protected…they were not wounded. You saved their lives. All of your students are safe."

Tears rolled down the side of her face. "Died… saw…" she mumbled, and closed her eyes.

"Yes, but you're not one of them. Your wounds were serious, but you're going to heal, and that's what matters. A whole lot of people have been praying for you. They are going to be ecstatic that you finally woke up," he said, and patted her arm.

The words *finally woke up* made her realize she'd been unconscious for a time.

She reached for her mouth. Her lips were dry. The words felt caught in her throat.

"How long...here?" she asked.

"Four days out of surgery," the doctor said. "Welcome back, Katie. Just rest. All you have to do right now is rest and get well, and I have the pleasure of going out to tell the media that you're awake."

———

They moved Katie from the ICU to a private room the next day, and Lila was right beside her all the way, quietly celebrating the knowledge that her best friend was still on this earth. As for Katie, she waited until the nurses finally left before she began questioning Lila.

"Are my kids all okay? What about Alejandro? Kieran?"

"They're all good. You saved their lives, Katie," Lila said.

Katie sighed. "Who was the shooter? Why did he do it?"

"A stranger. He'd only been in Albuquerque three months. No one knew him, and as far as I know, his reasons died with him."

Katie's voice was trembling. "I know Coach Lincoln died. He was right beside me when it happened. Who else?"

Lila's eyes welled. "Darrin Welsh, the security officer. Our principal, Mrs. Garza. Ellie Warren, who was one of the science teachers, and a little girl named Barbie Thomas—a fifth-grader."

"Oh my God," Katie said, and burst into tears.

Lila held her hand and cried with her. Being a survivor brought its own level of hell. The guilt of being alive.

Chapter 2

AFTER TEN DAYS IN THE HOSPITAL, KATIE WAS released.

Lila picked her up and took her home, made sure Katie was comfortable, and left to get her some fresh groceries.

Katie was propped up in her bed with a cold drink on the side table and an enormous pile of mail beside her. According to Lila, they were well-wishes from students and their families, as well as get-well wishes from strangers who'd heard about the shooting and her bravery and sent the cards to Katie in care of her school.

She lay there for a bit, staring at the pile of mail, and then closed her eyes, trying to make sense of what she was feeling. After being jilted, she'd slipped back into the old foster-kid mindset, wondering why she was never enough, why there was no one who wanted her, and as she grieved the loss, buried what was left of her dreams in her broken heart. But after she'd gone back to work, the passing days had moved into a maze of repetition that began to feel safe again.

Then the shooting happened, and when she took the first bullet, she was so afraid that she would die before she got the boys to safety. They were all that mattered. Now, knowing all twenty of her students had come through that horror without being shot was all she could have asked for. She would have gladly died to keep them safe, only the sacrifice had not been necessary after all.

There had to be a message in this for her.

Maybe she mattered more than she thought.

She mattered enough to still be breathing.

Her cell phone rang. She glanced at it, let it go to voicemail, and then got up and slowly walked through the rooms of her apartment. They were familiar. Nothing had crossed a boundary here that felt threatening. She'd been alone all her life. She could do this. She could get well here, but going back to bed was the first step. Her legs were shaky as she crawled into bed and began sorting through the pile of mail until she found names she recognized and began with those.

Some were from students she'd had in previous

years, some from parents, from staff and teachers at Saguaro Elementary, and many from people across the country. Some of them even had money in them, and all of them were filled with love and prayers.

There was a big manila envelope filled with messages and hand drawn pictures her students had sent to her. She knew them well enough to read between the lines. They were traumatized by what had happened to them and afraid she was going to die.

Katie was in tears as she put everything back in the manila envelope. Her students wanted to know when she was coming back, and she didn't know if she could. Just the thought of being back in those halls made her nauseous. She was scared to go back, and scared what would happen to her if she didn't. What if she was too messed up to ever work in public again?

She rubbed the heels of her palms against her eyes and leaned back against the pillows, trying to regain her equilibrium as she gave herself a pep talk.

This was her first day home from the hospital.

She was a long way from being healed.

Nobody was pressuring her to do anything, and she had a lot of sick leave built up, so she was still getting paid.

She would figure it out as she went, just like she'd done everything else, only not today. She fell asleep with a pile of letters in her lap and woke up when Lila came back with groceries.

"Hey, honey!" Lila said. "I got that prescription for pain pills filled. Do you need one?"

"Yes," Katie said, and started to get up.

"No, I'll bring it to you," Lila said.

Katie eased back against her pillows as Lila ran to the kitchen, grabbed the sack from the pharmacy, then raced up the hall again.

"Here you go. It says one every four hours, and no more than six in twenty-four hours. I'm going to put up your groceries."

"Thanks, Lila," Katie said, and was opening the container when Lila left the room.

Katie could hear Lila banging around in the kitchen and relaxed. Whatever needed doing in there, Lila had it covered.

Katie took a couple of pain pills, and then slid back down in the bed and closed her eyes. The sound of Lila working in her kitchen was comforting as she drifted off to sleep.

———

Lila began by cleaning out the refrigerator, dumping what was bad or out of date, and carrying out the garbage, then putting up the new groceries. When she had finished, she went back to tell Katie she was leaving, only to find her asleep.

She wrote a quick note, turned out the lights, and let herself out of the apartment.

Katie woke sometime later, found the note and food ready to eat in the refrigerator, and once again was so grateful for such a good friend.

She spent the rest of that evening going through the pile of mail. The notes were unexpected and heartwarming, except for one. Even before she opened it, she recognized the writing.

Mark.

She stared at it for a few moments, debating with herself whether she would even open it, then frowned and tore into it, pulled out a standard get-well card with religious notes, and a brief comment about how proud he was of her. She stared at the signature for a moment, wondering what the hell made him think she ever wanted to hear from him again, and then threw the card in the trash.

That night, she dreamed of the shooting and

woke up shaking, stumbled to the bathroom and threw up. Afterward, she made her way to the kitchen and got something to drink to settle her stomach. She was standing in the shadows with the glass of Sprite in her hand when she heard sirens in the distance and started shaking. It made her angry that the woman who'd given birth to her had chosen to abandon her in an alley, and that two men—one she'd loved and one she never saw coming—had come close to destroying her.

What the hell am I supposed to be learning from all this crap?

She took a sip of the drink in her hand and then walked to the window and looked out at the city below. The lights of the police car she'd heard were out of sight, but even at this time of night, the streets were still teeming with cars and people. Too many people. Too many loose cannons. She did not feel safe here. Not anymore.

She carried her drink back to the bedroom, took a couple more sips, and then got back in bed and turned on the TV. She finally fell back asleep with a Disney movie playing in the background, and woke up after 9:00 a.m. to find a text from Lila, reminding Katie to message her if she needed anything, and that she was bringing fried chicken and sides in time for her evening meal.

———————

And so Katie's self-imposed isolation and healing began.

They told her to take it easy and rest, and she was trying her best, even though it seemed as if the phone never stopped ringing. She kept wondering how people even got her number and decided someone in the school system had to have given it out. But if she didn't know the name that popped up, she let the call go to voicemail. It was her only defense.

She was mobile, to a degree, but still not released to drive, so she had groceries delivered, and sometimes food delivered, and the only person who came to see her was Lila.

As time passed, her isolation brought home to her how small her circle of real friends was, and she admitted most of that was her fault. She didn't want to be out and about.

However, the faux safety and comfort she felt during the day ended when the sun went down and the lights went out.

Then, the dreams came as she relived the panic, the pain, the horror.

Some nights she woke up screaming.

Some nights she woke up sobbing.

And every night when she went to bed, there was a subconscious fear that she would not wake up at all.

The toll it took on her physically and mentally was becoming obvious. Her clothes were hanging loose on her body now. Her face was thinner. She jumped at the slightest sounds. She was Zooming with a mental-health professional.

She'd survived, but at what cost?

———

Mark and Megan were living the high life. His new job was fulfilling, and while Megan wasn't exactly the homebody he'd expected of a wife, their time together was everything he'd dreamed it would be.

When Mark went to work, he left his wife in bed. And when he came home from work, she always had a beautiful table set and good food ordered in. It didn't even matter that she never cooked and didn't clean. She was pretty, and rich, and good in bed, and he knew she loved him.

And then the shooting happened at Katie's

school, and the fantasy he'd been living in began to deflate. As soon as he heard about it, he was in hysterics. He and Megan had their first fight about Katie. He wanted to go to the hospital to see her, and Megan told him if he did, not to come home.

Mark was pleading. He didn't believe her. "But Megan, it doesn't mean anything other than not wanting her to suffer alone."

And then Megan screamed and threw a plate all the way across the room, shattering it against the wall.

"No, Mark! You left her alone when you married me. She is no longer your business, and neither is her life. You're a fucking fool if you think she wants anything to do with you. Don't you understand that she probably hates you? She'll live or she'll die, whether you're there or not."

Mark was in shock. The woman screaming at him was a stranger. He'd never seen this cold, unfeeling side of her, and in that moment, something between them shattered.

He turned around and walked out of the room and didn't come back.

Almost immediately, Megan realized what she'd done and went after him. But it was too late. She saw the shock on his face. The damage was done.

"Look. I'm sorry that felt brutal," she said. "But you aren't seeing this from a woman's viewpoint. You betrayed her. She will hate you forever. And you're betraying me by wanting to rush to her side. How do you think that makes me feel?" she cried.

"Like an insecure bitch?" he asked, and closed the door to their bedroom in her face.

She gasped.

"I won't be talked to like this," Megan screamed. "I'm going to Daddy's to spend the night."

He didn't respond, and he didn't come out. Megan was furious, but at a loss. Instead of following through on her threat, she slept in one of the spare bedrooms and the next morning got into the shower with him and gave him the blow job of his life.

The fight was over.

But neither had forgotten what had been said.

The honeymoon was over, but the marriage was still intact.

———

It was a Tuesday in late May when Katie got an invitation she couldn't ignore. It was from Boyd French, the new principal at Saguaro Elementary, requesting her presence at a special assembly on

Friday to honor those who died, and the victims who survived.

The thought of it made her ill. But she needed to know if she could go back to that school and teach again, so she told him yes and didn't tell Lila. She could drive herself there. She could walk into that building on her own. After that, she made no promises, not even to herself.

———————

Friday came in a burst of sunshine in a cloudless sky the color of faded denim, with the Sandia Mountains delineating the space between heaven and earth.

Katie dressed with care, trying to minimize her waif-like appearance by wearing a long, pink-and-green-floral dress with a black background. The hem stopped midway between her knees and ankles, hanging loose on her slender body. The petal-style sleeves were comfortable, and the sweetheart neckline finished off the look. She chose plain black flats and wore her hair pulled back for comfort against the heat of the day, but her hands were shaking as she grabbed a small pink shoulder bag, then dug her car keys out of the bag, slipped on a pair of sunglasses, and headed out the door.

It was just before 1:00 p.m. when she pulled into the school parking lot and, when she got out, fell into step with a small crowd of people entering the building. She kept her head down and got all the way into the office without being stopped.

Michelle Aubry, the school secretary, looked up just as Katie was taking off her sunglasses, and burst into tears.

"Katie! Oh. I'm so glad to see you."

Katie sighed. *This is why I don't go anywhere. Everyone I see reacts like they're seeing a ghost.*

"It's good to see you, too, Michelle. I was summoned to attend an assembly. I assume it's in the gym?"

"Yes. They have a stage set up and the media is here, too, so prepare yourself."

"Oh lord," Katie said, and then a man came out of the office, saw Katie, and came toward her with his hand outstretched.

"Miss McGrath, I'm Boyd French. Thank you for coming."

Katie shook his hand and smiled. "Katie, please, and it's nice to meet you, sir."

Boyd French shook his head. "Believe me, the honor is mine. It didn't take me long to learn how much you have been missed. I'm not going to pretend this day will be easy for you, but you have no idea how beloved you are here. Your students ask me every day if you're coming back. I think they just need to see your face to know for themselves that you are well."

Katie's gut knotted. Guilt was a hard copilot, and knowing her children wanted her back made her feel sorry for them, and for herself.

"I'm looking forward to seeing them, too," she said.

"Well then, if you're ready, I'll be escorting you to the assembly," Boyd said, and then glanced at Michelle. "Call if you need me."

"Yes, sir," the secretary said, and then waved at Katie as the duo left the office and started down the maze of hallways to get to the gymnasium at the far end of the building complex.

There were dozens of people in the halls, all of them walking toward the gymnasium, chattering with each other and calling out to friends as they passed.

A sudden screech of laughter made Katie jump.

Classroom doors were banging as lagging students hurried to the gym to get into place. To Katie, it sounded like gunfire.

The first time it happened, she gasped, and for a moment, she was back in that day, looking for a place to hide.

Boyd saw her turn pale and slipped his hand beneath her elbow.

"I'm sorry. I didn't think," he whispered.

Katie shook her head. "It's okay. Just nerves," she said, then lifted her chin and focused on the cool air from the air-conditioning wafting down the back of her neck.

Boyd wasn't fooled. He'd done two tours in Afghanistan and Iraq, and he knew PTSD when he saw it. Katie McGrath was struggling. Maybe it would be better when they got out of the hall.

"We're almost there," he said quietly.

Katie nodded, blinking back tears. This feeling was awful. She was failing horribly. If she couldn't get down a school hallway, how would she ever be able to teach here again?

And then they reached the gymnasium. The bleachers were packed with students and families. The chairs set up concert-style out on the gym floor were for victims and their families.

Katie assumed she would be sitting there, until the principal led her up on the stage. The moment she started up the steps, she noticed cameramen from local news stations aiming their cameras at her. She was trying to come to terms with being the focus of attention when she heard little voices begin calling out, "Miss Katie! Miss Katie!" and lost it.

She made herself smile as she turned and waved, but she couldn't see the faces for the tears.

Boyd seated Katie next to him, handed her a program, gave her a quick nod, and then moved to the podium.

"Ladies and gentlemen, students, teachers, and members of the media, thank you all for coming. Six weeks ago today, a tragedy occurred here at Saguaro Elementary. A stranger came onto our property and shot his way into the building, causing great sorrow to all of us. This gathering is to honor and commemorate those wounded and those we lost, and thank you for coming."

The big screen above the stage was suddenly awash in color, with the logo of Saguaro Elementary, and as Boyd continued to speak, the images of those he began naming flashed on the screen behind him.

"As you all know by now, we lost our security officer, Darrin Welsh, a valued member of our staff.

He'd been with us for almost eight years, and he lost his life in a valiant effort to stop the shooter. Elena Garza, who had been your principal for thirteen years, called the police then ran out of her office into a blaze of gunfire and died. Coach Aaron Lincoln, who had been your soccer coach and history teacher, died trying to save children caught out in the hall.

"Ellie Warren, one of our science teachers, had already turned in her paperwork to retire at the end of this school year, and was shot and died in her classroom. And we lost Barbie Thomas, one of our precious fifth-grade students, who was looking forward to moving into middle school."

The silence within the walls was broken only by the sounds of weeping. Boyd French cleared his throat and continued, and so did the slide show, as he move on to the recognition of each of the twelve students who'd been wounded, and then the last picture was one of Katie.

"All of you…those who were not wounded, and those who were…those who we lost, and those who were saved, are heroes because you did everything right. It was the stranger who did everything wrong. But, in the midst of all the tragedy, first-grade teacher Katie McGrath shielded two of her students with her body, took the bullets meant for them, and saved their lives, and for that, we come today to also honor Miss McGrath. Katie, would you please come forward?"

Katie stood, her knees shaking. And as she began walking toward the podium, everyone in the gym began chanting her name.

"Katie! Katie! Katie! Katie!"

Boyd held up his hand, then pulled a plaque from a shelf beneath the sound system.

"Katie, on behalf of the Albuquerque public school system, and Saguaro Elementary, it is my honor to present this award. It reads: 'To Katie McGrath, for courage, bravery, and sacrifice in the line of fire.'"

He handed it to Katie, who was visibly over-whelmed as she clutched it to her.

"Are you okay to say a few words?" he whispered.

She nodded, then moved to the microphone and took a deep, shaky breath.

"Thank you. This is unexpected, and such an honor. But it feels strange to accept an award for doing the same thing every other teacher here was doing that day. We were all putting ourselves between your children and the danger they were in.

Every year, your children, who you entrust to our care, become ours for a little while each day. We work hard to make sure they are learning what matters.

"Some days we want to wring their necks. Some days we are so proud of them for how hard they try. And every day we love them. Enough to die for them, which is what happened here. I don't know why I'm still here, but all I can assume is that I am supposed to be. Again, thank you for this recognition, and thank you for the hundreds of letters and well-wishes that were sent to me."

The audience gave her a standing ovation as she walked back to her chair, wiping tears as she went.

The principal ended the program with a final announcement.

"Earlier this morning, we unveiled five wooden benches on the playground. Each bench has a name etched on it to commemorate a precious life that was lost here. Yes, the names will be reminders of our tragedy, but as time passes, the benches will also come to represent a place to rest from the innocence of play, and for teachers to sit while they watch over your children on the playgrounds. We will not forget.

"Now, this concludes our program. Students,

unless your parents are here, you will return to your classes. Parents, if you wish to take your children home with you at this time, they will be excused. Just notify their teachers before you leave with them. And…Katie, I think your class is going back to their room with their parents and teacher in hope that you will stop by to visit with them before you leave."

Katie nodded, but she was sick to her stomach. How in the hell was she going to get through this without falling apart?

———

Lila had known nothing about the award, or that Katie was coming to school, and when she saw her walking up on the stage, she could tell by the way she was moving that she was barely holding it together.

Every time in the past few weeks, when she'd mentioned coming back to school, Katie had gone silent, and now, seeing her like this, she understood why. It broke her heart to see her best friend so shattered again, but she knew in her gut that Katie McGrath would not be coming back.

She wanted to talk to her, but they both had other agendas. Katie was headed for her old class-room and her students, and Lila had to go back to the classroom with her students. She'd have to call Katie tonight.

———————

"I'll walk you to your classroom," Boyd said. "And if you'll call the office, I'd be honored to escort you back to your car when you're ready to leave."

"I appreciate your company to get me to my room. I'm sure I'll be fine to get myself to the car, but you have been so kind and…understanding."

He offered her his elbow, and she slipped her hand beneath it. Together, they made their way through the exodus of guests. They were about halfway there when Katie realized where they were and immediately looked down. When she did, she stumbled and would have fallen if the principal hadn't caught her.

"I'm sorry," Katie said. "I just realized where we were. It took me off guard."

"I don't know what you mean," Boyd said.

Katie shuddered and started walking, almost at a run, as if to get away from the area, and Boyd hurried to catch up.

"That's where Coach Lincoln was shot. We were running," Katie said.

"Oh my," Boyd said. "I'm sorry. I didn't realize."

Katie shook her head. "It's not your fault. Everything in this building triggers a memory now. It is what it is." And then they were at the door to her room. "I can take it from here," she said. "What's the substitute teacher's name?"

"Um...Abby King," he said.

"Thank you," Katie said. She took a deep breath and knocked, then pushed the door ajar.

There were parents lined up against the walls, and a short, thirtysomething woman wearing a yellow smock and purple pants standing beside the desk. She had a turned-up nose, pink hair, and a pencil stuck behind her ear. She looked like a living, breathing fairy. *How absolutely perfect*, Katie thought, and then smiled.

"May I come in?"

Abby King turned and opened her arms wide like she was going to hug her.

"Yes! Yes! Welcome back!" Abby said.

Katie waved at the parents and barely got the door closed behind her before she was engulfed. Twenty familiar little faces were turned up to her. Hands were touching and petting, and all of them were talking at once. And then she saw Alejandro and Kieran pushing their way through the crowd, and they were crying. When they got to her, they just wrapped their arms around her legs and held on.

Abby King immediately took control of the situation.

"Children, let's give Miss Katie a little room, okay? You will all get a chance to talk to her personally. Each of you find your spot on the floor in the reading circle, and Miss Katie can sit in the teacher chair, okay? Parents can listen in, but I think today is for Miss Katie and her class."

At that point, Katie put her purse and the award aside and dropped to her knees, hugging the boys to her.

"We thought you died," Alejandro said. "I'm sorry I fell down. You came back for us."

Kieran nodded. "You sure can run fast, Miss Katie. Thank you for coming back."

Katie knew if she cried now, everyone in the room would be in tears.

"Of course I went back to get you both, and Alejandro...everyone falls down. It's the getting back up that matters. And we all got up and ran, didn't we? And we're safe now. Okay?"

"Okay," they echoed, and then hugged her again. "We heard you tell us to not to talk and not to move, and we did just what you said," Kieran whispered.

"I'm so proud of you for following orders. It was important, wasn't it?" she said.

Alejandro nodded, then reached up and patted her cheek.

"You said you loved us. Just like Mama says when she tucks me in at night."

Katie's eyes welled. "And I do love you. All of you. You are so precious to me. Now. Let's go find our place in the reading circle, okay?"

They took off toward the circle as Katie followed, and then stopped at the desk where Abby King was sitting.

"Thank you, parents, for waiting so I can speak to your babies, and thank you, Ms. King, for letting me disrupt your class."

Abby smiled. "It's your class, too, and I'm just doing what I love. It's a pleasure and an honor to meet you. Now go sit down in your teacher chair and prepare to be grilled."

"Yes," Katie said, and slipped into her seat. For a moment inside that room, with all of the familiar faces of her littles, she almost forgot all of the bad stuff. "Okay, boys and girls, this is the last period before the bell rings, so each of you ask one question, and I will answer. And then if we have more time, you can ask more questions, okay?"

They nodded, and up went their hands.

Katie put hers in her lap so no one would see them shaking.

"I don't want to get mixed up with whose turn it is, so we'll just start here on my right with Dawson," she said.

The little redhead leaned forward. "Did it hurt to get shot?"

Katie's fingers curled a little tighter, but she kept the tone in her voice calm and even.

"Yes. It hurt then, but I don't hurt anymore. Karen, do you have a question for me?" Katie asked.

And so it went, until nineteen questions had been asked, and details added. When she got to Alejandro, who was the last student sitting on her left, she looked into his big brown eyes and saw fear.

"Alejandro, do you have a question for me?"

He nodded. "Miss Katie…are you coming back? Will you be our teacher again?"

Katie paused, choosing her words carefully without giving anything away.

"Well, as you know, the school year is almost over, so Miss Abby is going to finish out this year with all of you, and I can see from the amazing art on the walls and the happy faces before me that you all really like Miss Abby. Is that right?"

"Yes! We like Miss Abby," they chimed, and Katie flashed Abby a quick thumbs-up.

"So, when you come back to school after summer vacation, you won't be first-graders anymore. You'll be in second grade, and you'll have a new teacher. That's how school works, remember? You had a pre-K teacher. Then a kindergarten teacher. And then there was me, your first-grade teacher, and now Miss Abby. I'm all healed, but I don't have much 'pep in my step' yet, so I won't be back here before you go home for the summer. I'm still taking it easy at home. But I want you to know how much I loved having you in my class. And how much I love each of you, okay? Will you promise me to always listen when Miss Abby tells you something?"

"Yes! Yes! We promise, Miss Katie!" they cried.

Katie laid her hand on the top of Alejandro's head and then looked at the faces of the children before her.

"We all have people who come and go through our lives, but there will always be family and best friends. Now, it's almost time for the last bell to ring, and I know Miss Abby has things for you to do before you go. So I'm going to tell you goodbye, and maybe one day we'll see each other again. Now come give me a hug and go back to your desks."

They got up slowly, almost reverently, and filed past her, hugging her goodbye as they returned to their seats. Alejandro was the last in line, and when he hugged her, he whispered in her ear.

"I will be good. I love you."

"Oh, honey…you are such a good boy. I love you, too."

Katie got up before she burst into tears.

"Thank you, Miss Abby," she said as she picked up her purse and the award, then paused at the doorway before turning around. Everyone was watching her. She waved, and then she was out the door, swallowing back tears.

The hallway was empty, but she could hear clamor behind every door she passed as teachers were winding up another day on the job.

Her footsteps echoed, making her think there was someone behind her, and she kept looking over her shoulder, just to make sure she was still alone.

Her legs were shaking now. Her heart was

hammering so fast it was hard to breathe, and it was all she could do not to run. The office was just up ahead, and after that, the front exit, and then she'd be clear.

"Oh God…help me God…just a little bit further," she kept muttering, and then she turned the corner in the hall and saw the office in front of her, and then the front door to her left, and began counting off the steps to freedom.

One, two, three, four, five…ten, eleven, twelve… twenty-one…twenty-two steps! Take a left, Katie.

And she was out the door.

The afternoon heat was sweltering, and she was shaking as if she were freezing.

Shock.

Jesus wept. I am done.

Katie made it to her car, started it up, and drove away as if the devil was on her heels. The farther away she got, the more she began to relax, and the heat of the day began to seep into her bones.

She turned on the air conditioner and put the fan on blast as she moved into the traffic of the city.

It had been her day of reckoning, and she would never come this way again.

Chapter 3

THE MOMENT LILA REECE GOT HOME FROM school, she called Katie, but it went to voicemail, so she left a message.

"Hey, Katie, it's me. Call me back when you feel like it. I'm home for the evening."

Then she hung up and went to change before settling in with a stack of papers to grade.

Katie was on the sofa in the living room, wrapped up in a blanket against the blast of her air conditioner and watching a movie, when the phone rang.

When she saw it was Lila, she let it go to voicemail. She just wasn't in the mood to rehash anything right now. Being back in that school building had taken everything out of her that she'd fought to regain. She didn't know what she was going to do with the rest of her life, but it wouldn't be happening in that building.

Once her movie ended, she called in a DoorDash

order at Saggio's Pizza and then, while she was waiting for it to arrive, returned Lila's call.

The phone rang a couple of times, and then Lila picked up.

"Hey, girl," Lila said.

Katie grinned. "Hey, yourself. This is me returning your call. Do you have exciting news for me… like maybe that cute guy who lives down the hall finally asked you out?"

Lila groaned. "Unfortunately that is not the case. But I was hoping I could talk you into going to lunch with me tomorrow. We haven't had a girls' day out since you came home from the hospital, and I think it's time we did."

Katie surprised herself by agreeing. "That sounds like fun. I'd love that. Where and when?"

"Oh yay!" Lila said. "Let's do lunch a little early, say eleven thirty?"

"Works for me," Katie said. "Where are we going?"

"I was thinking Pappadeaux. I'm craving their seafood Cobb salad with shrimp," Lila said.

"Yes! We can get our Cajun on there, for sure! Okay, I'll see you there tomorrow."

Lila hesitated, then had to ask. "One other thing… Are you—"

Katie interrupted. "Yes, I'm fine...now. Yes, it was hard. No. 'Hard' is the wrong word. If I'm honest, it was awful going back. But I needed to see my kids. We all needed closure. They needed to see me alive and walking and talking, and I needed to tell them all goodbye."

"I guessed," Lila said. "So. We'll talk more tomorrow over good food and be grateful for the opportunity."

"Thanks," Katie said.

"For what?" Lila asked.

"For being the best friend I've ever had...for understanding...and for the invitation. See you tomorrow," Katie said.

"Yes, tomorrow," Lila said, and they both disconnected.

Lila was in tears. She felt her best friend pulling away.

But Katie was at peace. She'd faced a hurdle today, and while she might not have cleared it, it had become painfully obvious to her that she had to reconsider her options.

―――――

When Katie woke up the next morning, she stayed motionless a few moments, remembering today she was going somewhere fun with her best friend. She could be honest with Lila about her fears for the future, and maybe get a few good pointers along the way.

Finally, she got up and went to make coffee, then headed for the shower. She had a couple of hours before she was supposed to meet Lila, so she didn't have to rush. She stripped off her pajamas, wound up her hair and clipped it on the top of her head, then turned sideways in front of the full-length mirror to look at the healing wounds on her back.

One was on her shoulder, the other lower down on the other side of her back. Red, slightly puckered, still fragile skin was healing over the gunshots. Neither had an exit wound, which had been the blessing, or the boys might have been shot if the bullets had passed through her to them. But the extent of the surgery to get them out without damaging vital organs had slowed down her recovery.

She grimaced. Thinking about what-ifs was self-defeating, so she grabbed a washcloth and stepped into the shower. The jets of water hitting her body were warm and welcome, and by the time she got out, she was planning what she was going to wear. The predicted high today was in the 70s—sandals, summer blouse, and slacks weather.

A day for making good memories.

Mark had been cleaning the pool in their backyard all morning so that Megan could swim in it this afternoon, so he was hot and sweaty when he finally went inside. He took off his shoes in the utility room and padded through the house to their bedroom to clean up before he took Megan to lunch.

When he walked into the room, she was pushing a drawer shut in her dresser and jumped a foot when she realized she was no longer alone.

"Oh my God! You scared me. I thought you were still outside," she said.

Mark frowned. "I'm sorry. I'm going to shower, and then I'm taking you to lunch, remember?"

Megan took a deep breath and then smiled. "Yes, I remember. You clean up while I change, and then I'm going to finish that grocery list in the kitchen before we leave."

He nodded and went into the bathroom, turned on the shower, then stripped and got into the stall and grabbed the shampoo.

Megan's heart was still pounding at the close call, and as soon as she was certain he was in the shower, she began pulling open drawers, stripping what was taped there, and stuffing it all into a tote bag. Then she ran through the house and out into the garage and hid the duffel bag beneath a fake floor in the trunk of the car before dashing back inside.

Living a life of lies was harder than she'd expected it to be, but Mark was amazing in bed, loved her to distraction, and except for his continuing guilt about Katie McGrath, they were fine.

Now that she had the drugs and cash hidden, she dressed and then touched up her makeup before coming out.

Mark was half-dressed when he saw her, and the temptation to take off what he'd just put on was strong. But Megan's hair was done and her makeup was on, and he knew once she was primped, she did not like to be messed with.

"You look beautiful, darling," he said. "Where would you like to go for lunch?"

"I'm thinking Pappadeaux. It's been forever since we've been there. Does that sound good to you?" she asked.

"Sounds great," Mark said. "I won't be long."

A few minutes later, they were in the car and on their way across town, chatting about a golf tournament, the fall balloon festival, and what they were going to order.

Katie was a little late leaving her apartment, but once she got out of the building, the drive and traffic weren't bad. She was over halfway to Pappadeaux when her phone rang. She hit her Bluetooth to answer and kept driving.

"Hello?"

"Katie. This is Lila. I had a flat in the driveway. I called an Uber and I'm on the way, but I may be a few minutes late. Go ahead and get a table, and I'll join you when I get there."

"Bummer about the flat. I'll happily get the table and get some appetizers ordered. I'm starving. Do you have any requests?" Katie asked.

"Ooh…either crab cakes or fried calamari?" Lila said.

"You're reading my mind," Katie said. "See you soon," she added, then disconnected, braked for a red light, and then took a left on a green arrow.

A few minutes later, she pulled into the parking lot, glad they'd decided to come a little early because it was already filling up.

She grabbed her purse and got out, put on her sunglasses, and headed for the wafting aromas of Cajun cooking and seafood.

Once she was seated, she ordered fried calamari and iced tea for both of them, then settled back to wait for Lila to arrive.

It didn't take long before Katie saw her come flying through the front door and lifted her hand. Lila saw her, and when she reached the table, paused long enough to give Katie a quick hug, before sliding into the seat across from her.

"Thank you for ordering! Is this tea for me?" she asked.

"Yes, ma'am. Drink away," Katie said.

Lila took a quick sip of the cold drink. "That's nice. Maybe it'll cool down my stress. Lord. A flat."

"At least it happened while you were still home, or you'd be on the side of the freeway somewhere," Katie said.

"True. And AAA was changing out my flat in the driveway when I left. I'll take it to get fixed when I go home. Now...please tell me you ordered an appetizer already. I'm starving!"

"Fried calamari," Katie said.

"Yes! My fave. You're the best," Lila said.

Katie laughed, unaware the sound had carried across the dining area.

Mark Roman was absently listening to Megan's chatter when he heard that laugh. His heart skipped a beat as he looked past his wife's shoulder to where Katie and Lila were sitting and felt the blood draining from his face.

Megan had paused in her conversation and was waiting for Mark to respond when she caught him staring across the room.

"What are you looking at, darling?" she asked, and then turned around to look for herself. Almost immediately, she spotted Katie. "Well, hell. What are the odds?"

Mark sighed. "Yeah, what are the odds?"

"Ignore her," Megan said, and reached for his hand.

Mark frowned. "I feel like I should say something to her. I mean, she nearly died."

Megan glared. "You do *not* go speak to that woman!"

Mark's eyes narrowed. "We've already had this conversation. I will take orders from your father because he's my boss, but I do *not* take orders from my wife."

Megan blinked.

"Well, darling... Of course I did not mean to insult you. I just thought since the acrimony between you is so obvious, it would be in poor taste to disturb her. Especially since it appears she's having a good time with that woman."

"That's Lila, her best friend. They teach together," Mark muttered.

Megan swallowed the anger she was feeling. "Don't blame me if they dump their food on you," she said, and took another bite of her entrée.

Mark frowned. "She would never do anything that crass."

Megan didn't like it that he was defending Katie.

"Don't say I didn't warn you," she snapped, and swallowed the bite whole.

Mark was already regretting the urge, but if he backed down now, Megan would assume he was buckling under to her, so he headed toward the table where Katie and Lila were sitting.

———

The waitress arrived with the appetizer Katie ordered, took their orders for their entrées, and was walking away when Mark suddenly appeared at their table.

Katie was stunned.

Lila was livid.

Because Mark was nervous and uncertain how to begin such an awkward conversation, he just started talking in a genial, conversational tone.

"Katie, it's good to see you up and about. I just wanted to say what an amazing woman you are, saving those children like you did."

Katie heard him, then looked back down at her plate, popped another bite of calamari into her mouth, and started chewing without responding.

It was all Lila needed to see.

She waved her hand at him as if she were flicking away a fly.

"Get lost, dude. Your opinions and presence are unwelcome here."

Mark frowned. "I'm not speaking to you."

"And Katie isn't speaking to you, so beat it," Lila snapped.

"That's exceedingly rude!" Mark said.

Lila leaned forward, her voice rising. "No. Rude was what you did when you cheated on Katie, then jilted her at the altar and married the skank you were cheating with. You are a lying philanderer and you're in our space. Get lost, and if you think I'm kidding, I'm happy to start a great big fuss right here in the middle of Pappadeaux, and see how long it takes for someone to video it and upload it to their favorite social media sites."

Mark glanced at Katie, who was calmly dunking a piece of fried calamari in rémoulade sauce, then turned on his heel and walked away, well aware of the curious glances he was getting from the people who'd overheard their conversation. He hated to admit it, but Megan had been right, and she was waiting at their table with a smirk on her face.

"The waiter just came with the bill." She pushed it toward him. "Have a seat. You can't run yet."

Mark glared, pulled out a credit card and laid it on top of their tab, then grabbed his cell phone and began checking his texts so he wouldn't have to talk to her.

As for Megan, she'd just seen a side of Mark that made her nervous. He'd defied her. What the hell would he do if he ever found out about the Lanier family's side hustle.

―――――――

Back at their table, Katie swallowed her bite and grinned.

"You rock big time, my friend," she said.

Lila's cheeks were pink, and she was still livid.

"I swear, that man is clueless as hell. The absolute

gall of just strolling up and thinking we would be glad to see him."

Katie laughed, and again the sound rang out—all the way across the room to where Mark and Megan were sitting, still waiting for their credit card.

This time, even Megan heard it and wondered if they were laughing at her and Mark. She didn't like thinking she was the butt of anyone's joke, and stood up.

"I'll be waiting in the car," she said, and strode out of Pappadeaux with her head up and her hips swaying.

Several minutes later, Mark followed her out.

Lila had been keeping an eye on them, and once they were gone, she breathed easier.

"Well, Dumb and Dumber are gone, and here comes our food. Yum," she said.

Now that Katie knew she was no longer subject to Mark and Megan's presence, she relaxed. The rest of their lunch went undisturbed.

They were finishing up their meal when Lila finally broached the subject of Katie's future.

"Are you still going to teach?" she asked.

"Not in that building. I just can't," Katie said.

"Maybe in another school in the system?" Lila asked.

"I don't know, Lila. What I do know is I barely made it out yesterday. I wasn't sure if I was going to throw up or pass out before I got out of there."

Lila's eyes welled.

"I'm so sorry. That just breaks my heart. You're so good at what you do, and I love you to pieces, but at the same time I can't even imagine how you feel. I was standing at the locked door at my room, praying you'd come flying back knocking and shouting for me to let you in, and instead I heard shooting. When one of the bullets hit the door to my room, I hit the floor. I locked you out, and I will never forget that."

Katie pushed her food aside and grabbed Lila's hand.

"You did what you were supposed to do...what I asked you to do! You saved not only your class but mine as well. And I was never going to be able to get the boys back in time. That's why I threw myself on top of them. The shooter caught us out in the open. We're more fortunate than the five who died. And if the worst thing I have to live with is PTSD in school halls, then so be it. I may teach again, or not. I have to support myself, but I was a survivor a long time before this shooting ever happened...a long time before I got jilted. Okay?"

Lila sighed. She knew Katie's history. She got it.

"Yes. Okay. But you have to promise… Whatever you do, wherever you go, we do not lose touch with each other."

"Count on it," Katie said.

———

Mark and Megan's drive home was much quieter than it had been on the way to lunch, and as soon as they got home, Megan received a phone call from her father. They spoke, and as soon as they ended their conversation, she got up.

"I have to run over to Dad's house."

"Want me to go with you?" Mark asked.

Megan's stomach clenched. "No. This is your day off. I have every day off. Why don't you put on your swim trunks and lounge around the pool with something cold to drink? It won't take long and I'll be back to join you in the pool later."

"You sure? I don't mind," Mark said.

Megan threw her arms around his neck and kissed him.

"Yes, I'm sure. You're a darling. You worked hard all morning, and I'm sorry I was cranky. Go enjoy the fruits of your labor."

Then before he could argue further, she got her car keys, blew him a kiss, and hurried out through the kitchen into the garage where her Porsche was parked. She made sure the bag she'd locked up in the trunk earlier was safely stowed and took off in a rush.

It was delivery day at Daddy's, and she had something over eighty thousand dollars in that bag that she'd wanted out of the house.

———

After dropping Lila back at her apartment, Katie stopped off at a supermarket for groceries, and as she shopped, she thought back over her conversation with Lila. The weight of indecision was gone. Katie was not going to renew her teaching contract in the Albuquerque school system, and just acknowledging that released her from a mountain of guilt.

Within a week, she had turned in her resignation. A few days later, she received a personal letter from the superintendent of schools, thanking her for her years of service and expressing his sympathy for what had happened to her. He assured her that he would give her a glowing recommendation wherever she chose to go and wished her well.

Now that she'd officially resigned, she was free

to start looking into other options. She didn't have time to waste in deciding what to do because when her contract ended in June, so would her paychecks.

She began by making lists of jobs other than teaching and researching the qualifications needed. The biggest drawbacks were the pay scales and benefits. The jobs either had a decent wage but no benefits, or basic benefits but lower pay. It was a rude awakening. Between the nightmares at night and the uncertainty of her future, Katie McGrath was scrambling to find a foothold again. It was beginning to look like teaching was still, for her, her best choice, but she had to find a way to get past what had happened to her.

After looking online at Teacher Certification Reciprocity, she easily found out what was required in other states to be certified to teach there, then began ruling out anything farther west than where she was right now or in the northern states.

Then she began looking at job openings in small towns in the rural South. Once she was assured of certification in the states she'd chosen, she applied in rural areas of Texas, Tennessee, Oklahoma, Missouri, and Arkansas, and then settled in to wait for responses, while checking new postings every day for something else that might work for her. Everything about her life was in flux, which meant all options were open until she made a new decision.

Almost every night when she went to bed, she relived the shooting. Even when a dream started off on one subject, it morphed back to the school, and she would wake up in tears or hysterics. Katie's cheeks hollowed out from lack of sleep and weight loss, and the shadows beneath her eyes grew darker.

Emotionally, she was in prison—and she was her own jailer.

The first four responses from her applications came from multiple states. One from Arkansas. Two from Texas. One from Missouri. She immediately checked the pay scale to see where they fell within the parameters she needed, went online to research the towns they were in, then checked population and available rental properties before responding. Once the interview times were set up on Zoom, Katie began to feel optimistic.

The first Zoom interview was at 10:00 a.m. the next day, which happened to be on a Thursday. The open position was for a second-grade teacher in a small town not far from Hot Springs, Arkansas.

When it began, four people, counting Katie, were logged into the meeting. An elementary principal and two teachers were part of the interview committee. They'd barely made introductions to Katie before the principal, a man named Forbes, bluntly asked if she was the teacher from the school shooting in Albuquerque.

Katie was taken aback that the shooting incident, and not her qualifications, was the first subject of the interview because she had included that as part of her personal info when she applied.

"Did you not read my application?" she asked.

He frowned. "Yes, I read it, but—"

Katie was stunned. "So, you already know the answer, and yet you asked it anyway. Why?"

"I just wanted to get a feel for your emotional stability and—"

The callousness of the offhand comment made Katie's skin crawl. She cut him off without hesitation.

"Oh, my emotional stability is right where it always was…intolerant of rudeness and insensitivity. I'm ending this interview right now because I don't like what I'm feeling about your attitude. It makes me very uncomfortable. It no longer matters what you think of my qualifications because I withdraw my application. I have no interest in associating with your administration."

She disconnected herself, closed the lid on her laptop, and got up. She was so angry she was shaking. She'd expected questions about the shooting, but not confrontations just to see if she would throw herself into hysterics.

She was hurt, and disappointed, and struggling not to be discouraged.

The next interview wasn't until right after lunch. It was for a position as a first-grade teacher in an elementary school in a rural school district outside of Shawnee, Oklahoma. But after that first slap in the face, Katie was anxious. To kill some time, she traded her good clothes for shorts, a T-shirt, and running shoes, put on her Fitbit, grabbed her sunglasses, and left her apartment for a run around the neighborhood.

It felt good to be outside as she paused to stretch before taking off at a jog. Within a couple of blocks, she got lost in the impact of foot to concrete, the swish of her clothing as she ran, the sun on her face, the anonymity she felt behind the sunglasses.

But her endurance wasn't back in full force, so

she paced herself by jogging a distance and then walking, then repeating the process until she was back her apartment.

Katie was bathed in sweat, but she felt good— like she'd outrun the anger she'd left home with. She stripped, showered, and threw on a robe and went to the kitchen and dug through the fridge for the container of tuna salad she'd made last night. She got some crackers and a glass of iced tea, then turned on the TV and sat down to eat. She'd just taken a bite when she reached for the remote to up the volume on a news conference taking place.

The FBI was finally giving a statement regarding the shooting at Saguaro Elementary and the shooter himself.

Katie quickly turned up the volume and pushed her food aside to listen to Special Agent Baldwin, who was at the bank of microphones.

"...false name. He was living under the name Wilton Theiry, one of several aliases. His real name was Reuben Wyandotte Hollis, and he was born in Albuquerque in 1977. He was in and out of foster care here from the age of nine until he quit high school a month before he graduated. He had been living a transient life all over the lower half of the

States and had been in San Francisco for the past five years. The people we've interviewed who knew him indicated his continuing anger at what he called 'the system,' and said he blamed it for his inability to thrive in society.

"We don't know why he moved back to Albuquerque, or why he chose Saguaro Elementary as a target, but as far as we know, he had no personal connection to anyone there. As for what might have triggered him, it was discovered during his autopsy that he had stage-four liver cancer, so he may have chosen to end his own life this way before cancer did it for him. And like every other mass murderer, he chose people he didn't know to destroy. Finishing up this profile has ended our investigation. Do you have any questions before we end this?" he asked.

Hands went up as he glanced across the crowd of reporters and pointed at one.

The reporter immediately spoke up.

"Agent Baldwin, unfortunately, mass shootings have become almost commonplace now, and I've covered my share. But I've always wondered, why do mass murderers choose strangers? If they're angry with certain people, why aren't they the targets?"

Baldwin didn't hesitate. "Think about it. If they

don't have a personal agenda with certain people they want dead, then they choose strangers so they don't know who they're killing. They don't have any guilt or emotional connection to strangers' deaths. Mass murderers are not trying to punish those people they kill. They just want the world to see *them* and *their* purpose…*their agenda.* The dead are just collateral damage. And very few mass murderers expect to survive their personal rampage. They want to die in public. They view themselves as having not been 'seen' in life, but everyone will see them when they go down in a blaze of gunfire."

The questions continued, but Katie was done. She turned off the TV, so angry she was trembling. She knew the horror stories of foster care. She'd lived it. But she'd matured enough to know that there were some people who had turned their loss, grief, and rage into an identity. They took no responsibility for the troubles they had as adults and lived life as eternal victims. Getting cancer must have been what pushed the shooter over the edge.

She stared at the food on the table, then put the lid back on her tuna salad and returned it to the refrigerator. Right now, if she put another bite in her mouth, it was going to come up.

Instead, she took her iced tea out onto the little balcony off her bedroom and sat down in the shade to finish her drink. By the time she was through, her emotions had settled, along with her stomach, and she went back inside to get ready for the next interview.

Thankfully, the interview went well. The principal at that school was a middle-aged man, and the only one Katie spoke to. He never mentioned the shooting, which was a plus in Katie's eyes. It ended with the same speech about still interviewing applicants, and even if they were not offered the job, they would all be notified when the position was filled.

The next day was a repeat of the same. Two more interviews, these in Texas, both of which were less than promising. She had the feeling these people were going through the motions because that was required, and that someone within the school system was going to be offered the job. She didn't take it personally. That's how the system worked.

A couple more days went by, and Katie was constantly checking for new posts when she noticed one in a little town called Borden's Gap, Tennessee, that sounded promising. The opening was for a first-grade teacher. The pay was at the same scale as what she was receiving. Then she checked for rental properties and quickly discovered the one apartment building in town did not have vacancies, but there were small two- and three-bedroom houses for rent at a lower rate than what she was paying for her one-bedroom. So Katie filled out the application, sent off everything that was requested, and waited to hear back.

Acknowledgments

Hello to everyone,

I'd like to thank each and every one of my readers for continuing to support me through reading my books, talking about them with neighbors and friends, writing reviews and/or sending notes of encouragement to me. These stories were so much fun to write that I wanted to stay in that world rather than ending either of them. I'm also thrilled that Sharon Sala, a good friend of mine, has agreed to allow chapters of her book to be included.

A Chance Inheritance was only available in Audible, and *The Third Wish* was only offered in ebook format, and many of you asked for them in paperback. I'm so excited to say that your wishes have been granted. Happy reading to all of you!

Many thanks go out to Sourcebooks Casablanca and to my editor, Deb Werksman, for making this possible. Thanks also to the team there—Susie Benton and all the others who have worked so hard. As always, a special thanks to my agency, Folio Management Literary Agency, and to my agent, Erin Niumata. Also, to my family for understanding that sometimes I just have to write one more chapter.

Until next time,
Carolyn Brown

About the Author

Carolyn Brown is a *New York Times*, *USA Today*, *Wall Street Journal*, *Publishers Weekly*, and #1 Amazon and #1 *Washington Post* bestselling author. She is the author of more than one hundred novels and several novellas. She's a recipient of the Bookseller's Best Award and the prestigious Montlake Diamond Award, and also a three-time recipient of the National Readers Choice Award. Brown has been published for more than twenty years, and her books have been translated into twenty-one foreign languages.

She's been married for more than fifty years to Mr. B, and they have three smart, wonderful, amazing children; fifteen grandchildren; and too many great-grands to keep track of. When she's not writing, she likes to plot new stories in her backyard with her tomcat, Boots Randolph Terminator Outlaw, who protects the yard from all kinds of wicked varmints like crickets, locusts, and spiders.

Carolyn can be found on Instagram @carolyn-brownbooks, on Twitter @thecarolynbrown, on Facebook at facebook.com/carolynbrownbooks, and at her website, carolynlbrown.com.

Also by Carolyn Brown

What Happens in Texas
A Heap of Texas Trouble
A Slow Dance Holiday (novella)
Christmas at Home
Summertime on the Ranch (novella)
Secrets in the Sand
Holidays on the Ranch
Red River Deep
The Honeymoon Inn
Love Struck Café (novella)
Bride for a Day
Just in Time for Christmas

LUCKY COWBOYS
Lucky in Love
One Lucky Cowboy
Getting Lucky
Talk Cowboy to Me

HONKY TONK
I Love This Bar
Hell, Yeah
My Give a Damn's Busted
Honky Tonk Christmas